THE WILD ROSE

and other Prairie Parables

By David G. Johnson
Sketches by John S. Wilson

THE WILD ROSE and other Prairie Parables

Library of Congress Control Number: 2001119309

ISBN: 1-57579-232

Printed in the United States of America

PINE HILL PRESS
4000 West 57th Street
Sioux Falls, S.D. 57106

Dedication

For my wife, Glenice: good mother, grandmother
and faithful companion for 45 years.

For my two brothers:
Paul: 1938-2001, now golfing in glory.
and
Jerome: friend, too, and hunting companion.

Table of Contents

The Wild Rose 1

One of Us 5

Lund Drug Store 9

The Black Hills 13

Meet My Mother 17

When the Gate is Open 24

Speaking Up 27

A Bugle? 32

Fear 36

It's What You Know 40

The Hand Shaker 44

Jello 48

On Track 51

Out West 55

Representatives 60

"C.B." 64

Jake's Words 68

An Old Friend 72

The Rescue 76

Trouble In The Grove 80

Vic 84

Load Limits 88

Max 92

Forward

What would we do without stories?

As a preacher I had no choice when it came to stories. Use them or lose them (the first "them" refers to the stories; the second "them" refers to my listeners!). So, the preacher's life is one long search for metaphors, or illustrative stories and images. Stories help people to listen, to understand and to remember.

I have always liked that passage in Jeremiah 18, known as "The Potter and the Clay." God tells Jeremiah to go down to the potter's house and "there I will let you hear my words." As a matter of fact Jeremiah could have heard God's words anywhere, but they would not have sunk in as much anywhere else. In the potter's house he would receive a visual metaphor. He would know that God was the potter, and he was the clay.

Or, think of the powerful image Ezekiel projected in chapter 37, with his story of the valley of dry bones. Instead of merely telling the people that God would restore them, he paints the picture of the rattling bones coming together and of the strong winds sweeping down through the valley and breathing new life into the bodies. How could anyone forget God's promise?

Finally, there may not be a better illustrative story anywhere than the one Jesus told of the Prodigal Son. Jesus highlights the human conditions of rebellion and self-centeredness and, above all, God's great forgiveness and patience—or, as we say, God's grace.

All of our little stories pale in contrast to those great Biblical stories (and may others like them), but we need to catch the rhythm of scripture and continue its narratives in our own lives.

Aside from helping us to listen, understand and remember, stories remind us that God is in the real world. We often talk of inviting God into our lives. But God may be there already. Our task is to sense that and go with it. Celebrate it. Act on it.

I hope you will find these stories interesting, sometimes funny and inspirational and always respectful of life. Many of you who read my first two books, *Prairie Parables* and *The Road Once Traveled*, have encouraged me to do a third book. I hope you meant it because here it is, with as many blemishes and imperfections as has the one who wrote it.

John Wilson has provided some wonderful sketches to introduce each chapter, as he did in my first two books. I treasure John's friendship. He is a professional wildlife artist and it was kind of John to interrupt a busy painting schedule to make this important contribution. I suspect a few of you will buy the book for the drawings rather than the text!

In my 41 years in ministry I have served four congregations, Trinity Lutheran in Fowler, Colorado, East Side Lutheran in Sioux Falls, Lutheran Church of Our Redeemer in Watertown and Peace Lutheran in Sioux Falls. I have served as Lutheran Campus Pastor at two fine universities, The University of Kansas and The University of South Dakota. After retiring, it has been a great privilege for me to serve two congregations in Sioux Falls as interim Sr. Pastor, East Side Lutheran and First Lutheran. I thank all of the folks I have met over the years for their friendship and encouragement and recall fondly how we tried to help one another "keep the faith."

Our children have been a source of great blessing to us and I thank them for their encouragement to do another book. I am especially grateful to our daughter, Kari Mahowald, for proof reading the chapters and convincing me I need to use a few more commas. Other mistakes are probably due to my not listening to her. We are both Augustana College English majors, but don't blame the college for the mistakes either. I own up to them all.

Finally, I want to thank Jeanette at Pine Hill Press in Sioux Falls for her pleasing style and helpfulness. The people at Pine Hill Press are easy to get along with and do good work.

Dave Johnson
September, 2001

The Wild Rose

It may have a Latin name though it is hardly imperial. The Wild Rose, or Prairie Rose, is as common and unpretentious on the prairie landscape as a blade of grass. It grows in ditches, along fence lines and in pastures. It is a popular addition to any new shelterbelt because its rose hips make good food for the deer.

At least two states claim it as their state flower. Give it a fighting chance and it will thrive and spread in almost any kind of soil. It is not at all like its civilized cousins—the garden variety—that have to be cultivated, dusted, pruned, watered and otherwise fussed over endlessly. True, the tame ones do produce a magnificent flower and will last longer when picked. But, put them out along a pasture fence line and leave them on their own and see how long they will last.

The Wild Rose petals vary from a light to a deep pink. They are not flamboyant enough to have inspired much poetry but I have seen thick patches of wild roses that have brought a delicate beauty to an otherwise plain landscape. Harvey Dunn, the Kingsbury County painter of World War I and prairie scenes, titled one of his paintings "The Prairie Is My Garden." He depicted a mother with two children out on the prairie beyond their modest place gathering a bouquet of wild flowers. Depending on what time of the summer the gathering took place, since all wild flowers have their season, one would have to assume a part of that bouquet consisted of wild roses. Within a kitchen devoid of anything very colorful, the newly gathered wild flowers must have created a festive mood at supper.

The Prairie Rose is much like prairie people. They, too, are hardy, unpretentious, practical and, in their own way and time, striking. Most are neither famous nor infamous. They do, however, have a way of keeping their feet on the ground and living honestly and openly. Many are not extremely verbal, but it would be a mistake to equate this lack of verbosity with a lack of intelligence.

Prairie folks restrain their exuberance. The rains may come at the right time during the spring and the summer so that the crops appear unbelievably good. But ask a typical farmer how the crops look and the answer is likely to be "not too bad." I have thought of this prairie practice of understatement while reading the first chapter of *Genesis*. There it describes how God created the world in six days. At the end of each day God looked at what He had created and saw that it was good. If the author of *Genesis* had been from the prairies of South Dakota he would have written that God saw what He had created and it was "not too bad!" "Good" would have sounded too much like bragging. Not even God should brag.

Prairie folks have learned to be patient. If our folks, the schools or the church can't teach us patience, the weather will. Today the weather may be disagreeable, but just wait until tomorrow—or next week. It will change. In time, we become reconciled to the truth that we are just part of the total picture. The rain may have spoiled our backyard wedding reception, but the corn and pastures needed it badly. The March blizzard may have caused us to cancel travel plans, but the lakes and wetlands will be filled by the melting runoff.

As kids many of us also had to learn patience because of our wardrobes. Ever practical, my folks always bought my clothes a size or two larger than what actually fit me. They reminded me that I would grow into them in due time. I don't think there were rummage sales when I was growing up so my mother could not buy good used clothing. I was the oldest child in our family so it was my lot to get the new stuff, a mixed blessing considering the oversized attire bestowed on me. My brother got hand-me-downs but I think they fit him better.

I have thought of this practice in the course of teaching young people religion. The temptation is to always be relevant, to keep the class at the level of their immediate interest and talk about matters that fit them now. Naturally, most youth prefer that approach. But I have resisted, believing that while some of what I teach holds no interest for them at the present time they will grow into it. I'll admit that I have tried to answer questions they weren't asking. I have justified that because I believe that as their life experiences expand, the meaning of the faith will become more apparent to them. Just as our mothers forced a little oatmeal on us—something that would "stick to the stomach"—I have wanted to provide youth with something that would stick to the soul. We all crave immediacy but our prairie background counsels patience.

There is a kind of openness to prairie people. As the saying goes, "What you sees is what you gets." Aspiring to that myself, I felt complimented by one of my older granddaughters. Kimberly had done a paper in her science class in which she traced the progress of a sandwich through the body. Naturally, when the sandwich neared the end of its journey she had to deal with bodily terms and functions that we usually relegate to conversations in doctors' offices. Her father, a doctor, tried to tease her into giving a detailed report to all of us. Kimberly protested. I reminded her that God had created us the way we are, and assured her that our bodies are walking miracles. We shouldn't be ashamed of the way our bodies work, I counseled. A bit frustrated, Kimberly shot a glance at me and said, "Why did I know you would say that!" At least she did not accuse me of being overly subtle!

Given all of the technical advances to keep us comfortable and well, we prairie folks may have lost some of the hardiness of our ancestors. I look at the old family pictures and sense a toughness in those faces. Apparently, it was not considered appropriate to break into peals of laughter in front of the camera. Everyone was pretty sober. Beyond that, though, life required an inner strength to deal with the extremes of weather, as well as the fragility of life. Disease could decimate a family. Drought and insects might steal next year's food supply. Isolation was a fact of life and often led to loneliness and even depression. I have a friend whose grandparents came from Iowa to homestead in Harding County. His grandfather came first and tried to carve out a farm. Then his grandmother joined her husband. She did not get to town for seven years! Under those circumstances one would either melt away or draw from a deep well of fortitude. I see a survivor's strength in the faces of the early prairie pioneers. Does some of it remain in their ancestors? I would like to think they have produced children and grandchildren who can stand on their own two feet and face adversity. And, like the Prairie Rose, survive. Even with a bit of a swagger. Even with a smile in the face of a camera!

But, of course, these prairie pioneers were never alone. Just as the Prairie Rose survives only because of the rain, sunshine and fertile soil, the early pioneers knew from whence their sustenance came. Otherwise, how would you explain why Elling Eilesen, an early Norwegian pioneer pastor, in 1841, walked from Illinois to New York and back to secure an English translation of Luther's *Small Catechism?* That single journey symbolized the pioneers' conviction that their help came from the Lord. Transferring this life sustaining faith to their children was more important than passing on land, wealth or even dreams. It would be important to always "watch and pray," as Scripture advises. The prairie provided many incentives to do both.

One Of Us

The Sunday School Christmas program at First Lutheran Church in Sioux Falls had proceeded without a hitch. In fact, given the limited practice time for what was quite a production, the transitions from one group of participants to another were as smooth as silk. One of the reasons for this success could be found in the front pew where the director, with facial expressions and vigorous hand signals, directed the traffic.

But it all came unraveled with the sheep. That should not have been surprising since sheep in real life are fairly clueless. The little children were bunched up in the back of the church, all decked out in their wooly costumes, bleating vigorously. But, instead of moving down the aisle they stayed put. The teachers behind them signaled, throwing their arms forward like they were chasing a herd of real sheep. The director leaned into the aisle and gave ostentatious come-hither waves, like a third base coach waving the runner home. The sheep remained stationary. There were chuckles in the crowd. Now, at last, we had a genuine Sunday School Christmas program, where something always goes wrong. The kids were even cuter in their bewildered innocence. Finally the director got up and went back to the sheep. She gave them an encouraging smile and invited them to come with her. Without hesitation, they joined the director and came to the front of the church, turned and sang "Away In a Manger."

What a parable that turned out to be on the very meaning of Christmas, the Incarnation, or enfleshment, of God! Through Jesus, God came down to us to overcome our hesitancy and to walk with us into the Kingdom of God.

Over forty years ago I sat in the audience as Dr. Emory Lindquist, the president of Wichita University, spoke to a gathering of teachers. He said there were basically three ways to teach, and he used mountain climbing as an analogy. The teacher can point to the top of the mountain and challenge the student to climb to the summit. Or, the teacher can go to the top of the mountain and shout back down to the student a challenge to come up where he is. Finally, the teacher can stand beside the student, point to the top of the mountain and tell the student that they will climb it together. I guess I have had all three types of teachers, and I would agree with Dr. Lindquist that the best teacher is the one who shows enthusiasm for the quest and enters into the excitement of learning.

In the *Gospel of John* we read how the Word became flesh and dwelt among us, full of grace and truth. Someone once said that Jesus became like man so that man might become like God. That may be an oversimplification and may not bear up under the scrutiny of a careful theologian, but it captures a powerful truth. The Good Shepherd stays with the sheep out on the hillside and walks with them through the dangerous valleys and leads them to the refreshment of new pastures and cool waters. In time, he brings them into the sheepfold for protection during the long night.

The Christian story is an amazing one. To hear that the God who created the galaxies and put our planet together with a word would come to us as a gentle man and then submit to a humiliating and excruciating death is really so far fetched that we need help to believe it. When we say that the Christian Faith is a gift we mean the Holy Spirit has come to us and granted us the capacity to believe the story. For, after all, the wisdom of the world acclaims the whole story as nonsense. As Paul said, the cross is folly to the so-called wise.

My grandson had not been going to Sunday School very long when his folks asked him what they had talked about one particu-

lar Sunday. He responded, "Oh, it was about Jesus. It was a re-run."
Yes indeed! Isn't every Sunday really just a re-run? After all, what
else do we have to talk about? Sometimes we drift away from the
center and wander into peripheral themes such as social action or
church life or psychological "feel good" topics. But they aren't the
stuff of permanence. They aren't what has carried the church
through the ups and downs for centuries. The church is about Jesus
and how he talked about and lived out the love of God for all of us.
So we sing, "I love to tell the story of Jesus and his love." And we
focus on the cross.

If God had asked me for advice I would not have agreed with his
approach. I would have told God to come on strong. Make people
sit up and notice. Put on a little power play of some sort. I am a
product of an age that believes in slick advertising and effective
public relations. Maybe provide some divine version of a "blue light
special." Offer people a deal they can't refuse. But to rely on one
person who is chiefly known for his humility and then to place his
story in the hands of twelve untrained and often ineffectual disciples seems completely ridiculous.

Yet, would we have experienced any depth in our faith if God
had done it any other way? Would we have had any sense of God
understanding us or walking with us through the ups and downs of
life? We might have believed, but would we have trusted? One of
my favorite portraits of Christ is one painted by my Watertown
friend, John Wilson. It shows the face of one whose suffering has
produced not self-pity but great care for others. It shows the face of
one who has plumbed the depth of life with all of its pain and
trouble but is completely devoid of cynicism. It shows the face of
one who conveys an invitation: "Come with me." It shows the face
of one who compels me to answer, "Yes, I will come."

One of my favorite Christmas stories is one I have thought was
told by the Danish theologian, Soren Kierkegaard. In order to
include it here I have tried to find it in his writings. I even made a
call to a well-known Kierkegaard scholar. But I have not been able
to pin it down. So we'll give Kierkegaard the credit, God the glory
and tell it.

The wife of a Danish farmer and her children prepared to go to
church for the Christmas Eve service. Her husband did not see
much to get excited about in the Christmas celebration so he
decided to stay home. As he sat alone at home the wind came up
and the temperature dropped dramatically. He heard other noises
than the wind outside so he peered out the window. There he

observed a number of birds in the bushes by the house and in adjacent trees. They seemed to be seeking shelter as they shivered in the cold wind. He felt sorry for them. He put on his jacket and went outside to open the barn door so they could fly in. Then he went back inside and looked to see if they would accept his offer. They would not. So the farmer proceeded to take some crumbs from the kitchen and sprinkle a path from the trees into the open barn door, hoping they would feed themselves into the shelter. But their fear was greater than their hunger and that did not work either. Frustrated, he grabbed a broom and attempted to chase the birds into the barn. That only caused them to scatter in every direction where there was less shelter than what they had. He knelt in the snow, talking to himself. "If only I could become one of them then I could bring them into the barn." Just then he heard the church bells signaling the beginning of the Christmas Eve service. As he knelt there in the snow the meaning of the incarnation of Jesus dawned on him and he prayed, "Thank you, Jesus, for becoming one of us, so you could lead us to safety."

Lund Drug Store

It really was a corner drug store. It stood on the busiest corner of Oldham with a bank across the street to the north and a bar across the street to the east. If the streets in Oldham had names I was not aware of it. I don't believe Lund Drug had an address other than town and state. It didn't matter. Everybody knew Cecil and Elsie Lund and where to find their store.

If you were looking for someone, Lund Drug was among the two or three places to check. It was popular with people of all ages, partly because you could satisfy a variety of needs there and also because Cecil and Elsie made everyone feel welcome. The only visitors to town Cecil did not welcome were the referees at the basketball game who didn't show a marked favoritism towards the Oldham Dragons. He would sit on the stage overlooking the gym and boom his opinions across the floor, all of which could be summed up as an invitation to leave town as quickly as possible, preferably before he had a chance to get hold of them. Cecil was one of several in town who took high school basketball seriously. For many the stature of the town rose or fell depending on the record of the Oldham High School basketball team. I will never forget how Cecil and Elsie took me along with them to Brookings to watch South Dakota State play basketball. They had no children of their own and were kind to other kids too.

The Lund Drug Store remains vivid in my memory. It is gone now, having been replaced by a new bank, so that unique corner of my hometown and my life has to be recalled instead of seen. A tour of the store these days requires some imagination and three stops.

First, there was the display window. I think Elsie, or one of the girls who worked there, was in charge of designing the displays in the window, which faced the main street to the north. It may have been the only store in town that tried for any kind of artistic arrangement of advertising. Most of the stores used whatever display area they had as additional storage space. But in the Lund Drug window there were seasonal arrangements, generally some Fenn's Ice Cream ads, a few comic books and other enticing items meant to lure a customer into the store. I don't mean to suggest it had the pizzazz of a Fantles or Shriver Johnson department store in Sioux Falls, with electric trains, stylishly attired manikins and all the other kinds of glitter and glitz the fancy stores displayed. It wasn't fancy, but it was nice and more than adequate as an invitation to come in to the store and have a look around. With that kind of attention to detail people could sense this was a proud business and one that wanted to contribute to the ambiance of our main street as well.

Second, there was the store itself. When you entered through the door on the northeast corner, the magazine rack was right there to your right. There were always lots of comic books. We read many of them on the rack so they were often well worn before they were sold or taken back by the distributor. One of the magazines on sale was, of course, *Life* magazine. That provided us with a little attempt at cleverness. "What is life?" "Five cents." "What is five cents?" "Life." And so on. That was our local, more easily remembered, version of "Who's on First?" It seemed more brilliant then than it does now!

The marble soda fountain stood against the west wall. It was the source of sweetness and delight. Little did I realize, when I had my last lemon cherry phosphate there, that it would be my last one ever. Other favorites included ice cream cherry sodas and huge dips of butterscotch revel ice cream in a cone. More often than not we would conclude a day at school by heading for the drug store for what we considered a well deserved treat for having survived another day of education. Aside from the old fashioned ice cream tables and a couple of booths where we would sit and try to pro-long the ecstasy of our purchases—much like an opium den in other cultures—the store contained shelves of items for personal use or gift giving.

As a seventh grader I had a girl friend. I had won enough marbles from her during the summer to bring out a little guilt at Christmas. Somehow we conveyed to each other the notion that we should exchange gifts. So I went to Lund Drug to find a suitable present—one that would suit her and my limited budget. I bought a compact for her. She bought a scarf for me at the same place. I was a little embarrassed about the matter and never intended to tell my folks. But the adult grapevine was more effective than I realized and my folks found out about it even before I had given the gift to my girl friend. I thought they laughed a little too heartily. Was having a son in love that funny I wondered?

Cecil and Elsie, and occasionally a sister-in-law, Nina, dispensed drugs from the counter in the back of the store. Cecil was as close to being a doctor as it got in Oldham. He would often bind wounds and give out medical advice, a practice to be avoided like the plague in today's litigious society. There may have been doctors closer, but ours was in Brookings, thirty-three miles away, and having Cecil close at hand was a comfort.

The third stop on a tour of Lund Drug would be in the back room. I say this with some pride in that there weren't many who ever got back there. But Cecil had hired me to come down to the store every Saturday morning to burn trash. By then the back room would be full of empty boxes and ice cream containers. The whole room was a mess. The floor was sticky from melted ice cream and various kinds of debris were scattered hither and yon. I hauled the residue of the week's business out to the wire cage in the back and set it on fire. Cecil instructed me to stay by the fire, once I got it going, so burning scraps would not start blowing around. That was not tough duty because even in the winter I had a nice source of heat. Then I swept and mopped the back room floor and prepared it for another week of mayhem.

It has struck me more than once how much like the Lund Drug Store we are as human beings.

We have our display window where we present ourselves in the best possible way. Our fantasies produce at least two persons, the one we think ourselves to be and the one we would like others to think we are. We all know the self we present to the world around us is not always a true reflection on what we are thinking or feeling, but it is a fact that all of us want to present an image that more closely approximates the ideal rather than the real.

Then there is the store itself where we do the real business of life. This is who we actually are. In the give and take of life we have our ups and downs. We come to terms with our weaknesses and our strengths. We have some successes and some failures. In the course of living the world manages to knock off some of our rough corners and our goal of bringing pleasure and meaning to others is occasionally realized. Sometimes we are dreadfully busy. Other times we coast and have time to ponder the transactions of life. On balance, we hope there are more gains than losses.

Fortunately there is also a back room to our lives. It's the place into which we throw the empty and the messy leftovers of living. We really don't want anybody to go there since it is the place we toss whatever it is we want to get rid of. Sometimes it gets very cluttered. Hopefully, we have found SOMEONE who can come in and carry all the debris out and burn it. If not, it will soon spill over into the areas where we live and move and begin to mess up the public part of our lives.

This back room also symbolizes who we can become. Emptied of our garbage and cleaned we are ready for more living. It could even be that over time there will be less trash to destroy. But we won't count on it.

The Black Hills

I love the Black Hills. I go there whenever I can—to camp, hunt, fish or bike. When our children were young we almost always pulled our camping trailer to the Black Hills where we had a favorite campsite. It was about as far as I cared to drive with four lively children. Aside from the natural beauty of the Hills, there are all kinds of family activities available that don't cost anything. We saved a few of the tourist attractions for rainy days. Our children are grown now and have their own families, but they continue to gravitate towards the Black Hills for their family outings, unable to resist all the fond memories they carry from days gone by. It is nice to have a place like the Black Hills National Forest that belongs to every American.

I have enjoyed reading about the history and the geology of the Black Hills. In either case there are lessons with very human dimensions to be learned, aside from the actual facts, which are important too.

One of the more fascinating books on the history of the Black Hills comes from an eyewitness account provided by Annie Tallent in her book, *The Black Hills or the Last Hunting Grounds of the Dakotas.*

In 1868 the Black Hills was a part of that vast tract of western land ceded to the Indians. But it was not long after the cession that rumors began to filter back east about the probability of gold existing in the Black Hills. The lure of gold was irresistible to many and soon groups of people began making illegal forays into the Hills. Annie Tallent was a member of the first group, which began the journey from Sioux City in 1868. They headed straight west and then came up into the Hills from the south, through Indian country. They exerted every effort to avoid encountering Indians, although the resistance of the Indians was not as strong or organized as it would later become. Their chief concern was to avoid being detected by government troops whose assignment was to intercept the parties heading for the Hills. Failing to do that, the soldiers were commanded to evict any settlers who made it to the Hills. Tallent's party succeeded in getting to the Hills through some devious maneuvering through the Badlands, at one point hiding behind one side of a butte while the soldiers rode on the other side. Eventually government soldiers found them and evicted them from the Black Hills.

It was a losing cause for the United States government, although the troops did catch one party and attempt to demonstrate they meant business. They halted the party of gold seekers, burned their wagons and the contents and sent them packing back to Yankton. That would not be enough to cure the gold fever

Even before 1877, when the Black Hills was ceded back to the U.S. government, the government changed its policy. For one thing, there was no way of stopping all the adventurers who were now streaming into the Hills. Also, after the defeat of General Custer in 1876, the Indians had become more militant and better organized under Chief Crazy Horse and other leaders. They constituted a very serious threat to the settlers. There was also a growing number of highwaymen, outlaws and other ne'er-do-wells who were making the Black Hills a dangerous place to visit or live.

Now the attitude of the settlers towards the U.S. military changed completely. Whereas before they had resented the troops and tried to avoid them, now they eagerly sought their presence and celebrated their arrival. When, in 1876, General Crook fought his way from Bismarck to Deadwood to help protect the pioneers, the residents of Deadwood gave him a fabulous reception. This shift in attitude did not take long, given the precarious nature of life in the early days of Black Hills settlement. When the early settlers were intent on doing what they wanted to do, even though forbidden by their government, the adventurers regarded the troops as a threat. Later, when their situation proved alarming and they were afraid for their lives, they saw the troops as their salvation and welcomed them into their midst enthusiastically, even though they brought with them the authority of the U.S. government. Or, maybe, it was precisely because they brought with them this higher governmental authority.

Such is the path many of us have trod in our response to authority. There is something in all of us, associated primarily with youthfulness but we are never totally without it, that wants to do whatever we choose. We resent authority. We crave freedom. Having spent roughly a quarter of my 41 years of ministry on college campuses, I have observed young students who are for the first time in their lives away from the restraints of home. Many are anxious to take maximum advantage of this new freedom and, in the process, misuse it. Some never recover and their college careers either come to an abrupt halt or they flounder until they discover there is no freedom without self-discipline and observing the disciplines of academia.

Actually I don't believe there is such a thing as raw freedom. If people are free to do anything they please then nobody is free, including those who are supposedly exercising their freedom. As the saying goes, "Your freedom ends where my nose begins." You can flail your arms in the air all you want to but not in such a way that you belt me in the nose. I think that may be the point of the Ten Commandments, given to the Hebrew people on their forty year journey from Egypt to the Promised Land. It's as though God was preparing them for the new freedom they would now experience, having endured all of the cruelties of slavery in Egypt. God did not want them to slip into a different kind of bondage where nobody would be free because everybody did what he pleased. So God commanded them to recognize Him as their authority and placed restraints on what they should or should not do to one another. Only by accepting this authority would they remain free.

The second lesson of the Black Hills comes from its geology. I am indebted to Sven G. Froiland, who taught biology at Augustana

College for many years and up until his retirement served as Director of the Center For Western Studies on the campus, for the insights he provided in his book, *Natural History of The Black Hills.* I am by no means an expert on mountain building, but I understand the Black Hills, older than most mountains, were formed by "updoming." Because of some sort of weakness, or perhaps resilience, in the earth's crust the mountains were able to push up at that point rather than somewhere else. A combination of erosion and uplift over millions of years brought into being one of the most beautiful places on the entire earth. Born in weakness, one might say, the rugged and rocky mountains now exude strength and force.

Isn't that exactly what St. Paul is talking about in *2 Corinthians* 12:10? He says, "For the sake of Christ, then, I am content with weakness, insults, hardships, persecutions, and calamities; for when I am weak, then I am strong." Paul cites those conditions commonly thought of as weaknesses and points out how he is then more inclined to rest in God's strength, thereby achieving a power beyond anything he could muster on his own. The overall impression I have of Paul is one of uncommon ruggedness and boldness. He would say that is because his weakness allowed God to do some "domebuilding." And God built a majestic mountain called St. Paul. "It is no longer I who live," he proclaimed, "but Christ who lives in me."

When you carry the lessons of the history and geology of the Black Hills into life those ancient and beautiful mountains, so awesome to behold, provide one echo after another of deep and abiding meanings.

Meet My Mother

Scripture tells us that God is love, one of the few so-called definitions of God found in the Bible. The story of Jesus is an account of God's love in action. It is a powerful love story, evoking a loving response from us when we hear it clearly and perceive that we are the objects of God's love.

But there are many other evidences of God's love for us, not always spelled out completely in the Bible, though there are scattered references here and there. Surely one of the major ways God brings his blessings to us would be through the countless ways we are nurtured and helped to achieve wholeness. In other words, God has provided that we should all have mothers.

Our mothers have not only brought life to us but also have given us care and counsel without which we would be hopelessly deprived, even arrested, in our development. Mothers are fountainheads from which flow riches and resources that carry us through growth into maturity. We are deeply indebted and much devoted to them.

I have had at least four mothers and I would like to introduce you to them, with a hope that my maternal ties would reflect that of many others.

First, I would like to have you meet *Mother Goose*. Remember all those little nursery rhymes we heard and memorized as children and how proudly we repeated them when asked. It was more than an exercise in showmanship or a boost to parental pride, though it was all of that. Those little rhymes, with their mixture of realism— even violence, sometimes—and fantasy, contained bits of wisdom and common sense that prepared us for life.

There was the misfortune experienced by Jack and Jill.

> "Jack and Jill went up the hill
> To fetch a pail of water.
> Jack fell down and broke his crown
> And Jill came tumbling after."

Both Jack and Jill were being good and obedient, no doubt responding to a request from a parent to help with the chores. Yet something horrible happened to them. Breaking one's crown has got to be serious, certainly more than a mild concussion. And I would suppose the only reason Jill fell down was that she was trying to help Jack, either with lifting the pail or trying to interrupt his fall. So, very early on in life, we learned that bad things happen to good people, often through no fault of their own. In a far more profound way the Old Testament book of *Job* deals with the same question. Job, a good man, experienced all kinds of terrible calamities. Thus, through 40 chapters, the gist of Job's complaint (he was not a patient man!) to God is: Why must the righteous suffer?

Or how about the wisdom of Little Bo Peep?

> "Little Bo Peep has lost her sheep
> And doesn't know where to find them.
> Leave them alone and they'll come home,
> Wagging their tales behind them."

If I recall correctly the solution offered to Little Bo Peep has been useful in governmental affairs, where we call it "benign neglect." For that matter haven't we all told one another, "just leave it alone and everything will work out ok?" Sometimes we do better by not trying to fix everything. We might make it worse. People have been known to try to dig themselves out of a hole, after an inappropriate action or comment, and they only make the hole deeper. The Beatles sang the song, "Let It Be," and sometimes that is the best thing we can do. Hopefully it worked that way for Little Bo Peep!

One of my favorite rhymes as a kid was about Humpty Dumpty's fall.

"Humpty Dumpty sat on a wall
Humpty Dumpty had a great fall.
And all the king's horses and all the king's men
Couldn't put Humpty Dumpty together again."

There are some accidents that are irreversible, in spite of good intentions, ingenuity and power. The *Puritan Primer* explained human sinfulness with the rhyme, "In Adam's fall we sinned all." And Scripture tells us that our brokenness cannot be repaired even by our best efforts. Only God, through his forgiving love, can make us whole again. I have met Humpty Dumpty and he looks a lot like me.

Eventually we leave Mother Goose behind, or should I say she takes ever new forms, for we are always in need of the nurturing influence of wisdom. We go to school and find that Mother Goose has not abandoned us. She now comes to us through the insights of novelists, playwrights, artists, historians, musicians, theologians, scientists and others who pass along wisdom to us. It is no wonder that we refer to our schools as "alma mater," which means "fostering mother." My college, like most, has a hymn called "Alma Mater." It is a hymn that I have sung many times and now that I am nearly forty-five years past my graduation and have what is called historical perspective I am impressed with its words.

"Augustana, we sing out thy praises,
Our hearts overflowing with love.
As thy banners we bear, we willingly share,
The gift that was given from above.
We cherish thy aims and traditions.
To thee we will ever be true.
As we march on through life,
We'll let love o'ercome stife,
Thanking God Augustana for you."

Referring to an institution of learning, whether it be a high school, vocational school or college, as a fostering mother issues from a time honored practice of referring to wisdom in the feminine gender. In *Proverbs* 4:6 we are advised to never let go of her apron strings: "Do not forsake wisdom, and she will protect you; love her, and she will watch over you."

We come into this world knowing nothing. It's a good thing that Mother Goose and her colleagues, some with graduate degrees, are willing to impart knowledge and wisdom to us all through our life, informally first at our mother's knee, then formally in the schools we attend, and then informally again as we make our way through life.

The second of my mothers whom I would like the reader to meet is *Mother Nature*. If Mother Goose nurtures our minds then Mother Nature nurtures our spirits. We draw inspiration from the beauty, power, rhythm and miracle of creation. Of all our mothers, this one is the most flamboyant, with an Irish flair for theater, but also sometimes displaying the temper of a wounded bear. We even speak of having to tame her, since there is a natural wildness to her works and ways.

Thomas Jefferson offered the conviction that no one should ever be president of the United States who did not have a history with the soil. Only in a truly agrarian setting could those values which nature held become self evident, he believed. To lose contact with the natural world was tantamount to losing contact with the source from which we draw our morals and a good deal of inspiration. Most of the earliest presidents were, of course, just that—farmers. Of those early presidents, John Adams was the most hands on farmer of them all. Perhaps that explains not only his solid character but also his enormous patience with the French, the Dutch, the English and with Thomas Jefferson and his anti-Federalist friends. After all, farmers learn that you can't make the beans grow by going out and pulling on them.

I like Mother Nature any time of the year. In each of the seasons on the Upper Great Plains she offers a gracious invitation to spend time out of doors. She teases us in the spring, which always seems to come too slowly. We are infected with a touch of cabin fever and become anxious to get out to plant and fish and play golf. But just when we think winter is over it comes back, unpacks its suitcase and lingers for awhile. Soon the calendar wins and the grass turns green, the leaves begin to sprout, the tulips bloom and the birds return to provide the music we missed in the winter. Even before there is any serious yard work to do we look for excuses to be outside.

Summer settles in then and we relish the mornings and evenings most. There is color all around us and gardeners are in their glory.

When we travel we gravitate towards those areas of pristine and natural beauty—the lakes, mountains and forests. For most of us these are places of renewal or re-creation.

Fall sneaks up on us. I wish fall was a genuine season. Then it might last longer. As it is, fall is more a time of transition than a season. But what a glorious couple of months it is as the grasses, shrubs and trees take on earth tones, the moon comes up red, a haze settles on the late afternoon, golden landscape, the harvest is brought home and hunters take to the wetlands and uplands with eager dogs. An unforgettable part of growing up in a small town is the smell of burning leaves in the air. Sometimes you can still catch that wonderful aroma if you go to the right places.

Winter is sometimes too long and too cold, but otherwise it can be an invigorating time of the year. I like the sharpness and the quiet of the season and rarely miss an opportunity to take a walk. Having a large dog that needs the exercise helps me get out when the flesh is weak. Aside from the opportunities to enjoy the snow, winter flavors our life indoors too. It makes our homes cozier and we are inclined to read, listen to music and indulge other indoor interests more during the winter than any other time. Some of our reading may include an early catalogue of things to plant in the spring. And so the seasons come, around and around, and we are the better for having experienced each one.

Mother Nature is indeed a nurturing mother. She fills our life with glorious sights and sounds and lifts our spirits. Even in the concrete chasms of a city it is not uncommon to see protruding out of a 10th floor apartment window a box full of bright flowers. The human spirit craves the presence of this mother. We never outgrow our need for her.

The third of my mothers is *Mother Church*. Perhaps this mother is the one against whom we have rebelled the most. We have thought her to be heavy handed, old fashioned, out of date or sometimes indifferent to our needs.

But it is the church that has consistently been the fountainhead of grace. She is not the moralistic matron we may have imagined her to be. If she has been overbearing she was not being true to her nature. She has washed us clean in baptism and marked us with the cross of Christ forever. She has brooded over us in our infancy through the Cradle Roll program of prayer and helpfulness to parents, she has taught us the great Bible stories in Sunday School and the teachings of the Faith in confirmation classes. She has given us great prayers to pray and hymns to sing. She has erected pulpits from which God's Word is brought to bear on our souls and daily lives. She has invited us to her altars to kneel and be hugged by God through the gift of Holy Communion. When we marry we come to her for a blessing on our vows and our new family. When we experience the ups and downs of life we ask for her prayers. And when we breathe our last we ask her to speak the promises of God over our remains. We appreciate the sense of family within her household and the gift of brothers and sisters in Christ. Truly, she is like a mother to us from the beginning to the end.

Mother Church fills many roles. She is like a nursery in which the seed of faith is planted, like a school where we are taught the fundamentals of the faith, like a shrine where we come to praise our God, like an arena in which we fight the good fight of faith, like a hospital in which we are healed, like a training camp where we are prepared for service and like a launching pad where we are lifted into glory.

As a parent, knowing that I won't be around forever, it gives me comfort to see my children and grandchildren finding their place in the church. I am glad they will experience the same mother I have known—Mother Church.

Finally I would like you to meet my mother, *Esther*. Since she passed away in 1976 it will not be possible to meet her in the usual way. Nor do I plan to present a complete word picture. Rather, I suggest that others think of the mothers they know best—their own.

Our mothers gave us birth and if that were their only contribution that would be enough to claim our devotion. But they have gone so far beyond that initial contribution that we almost overlook the biological side of motherhood. They fed us, kept us clean, listened to us, taught us our first and most basic living skills, corrected us, challenged us, punished us and forgave us. There were moments (maybe even long stretches) in our lives when only God and our mothers could love us. Both did.

We remember special qualities peculiar to our own mothers. I asked my brother what he remembered about our mother. He said it was her patience. I told him that was because he required more of it than I did! He recalled one time when mother got a report that the coach had scolded the kids for smoking. She heard that one boy, Michael, appeared to be quite uncomfortable as the coach told of how his wife had seen some of the boys smoking as she looked out the back window of their home. Mother heard this in the presence of my brother and other women. She said, "Why Michael and Paul are almost always together and what one does the other does." Then she turned to Paul and asked, "Were you smoking too?" Mother was cutting Paul's hair at the time and he answered in a breaking voice several pitches higher than usual, "no-o-o." She spoke to the women who were there, "I can always tell when Paul is telling the truth." She never said another word about it, thinking maybe he had been made to squirm enough. She knew he knew she knew!

A mother's love is a mixture of worry, hope, disappointment and joy. The physical pain our mothers experienced in our delivery probably paled in contrast to the emotional pain we caused them as we grew up. But they stuck with us through thick and thin and for that we owe them our most profound gratitude.

In fact there is a very short and direct line between thoughts about any of our mothers and a deep sense of gratitude. We are reminded that we have warmed ourselves by fires we did not build and drunk from wells we did not dig. If God should ask us to count the ways he has loved us, the gift of our mothers would rate very close to the top.

After an all too brief visit our daughter, her husband and two children left for home in their relatively small vehicle. Anna, who just turned four, sensing they were crowded, said to her mother, "Where will my kids sit?' Her mother explained to her that when she had children she would have her own car. "No," she said, "they will be with me right here." She repeated the question at bedtime. "Where will my kids sleep?" She refused to believe she would have her own home. She was not yet ready to entertain thoughts about leaving her parents and yet she had already begun to fathom some motherly instincts in her concern over the well being of her future children. So here is God at work again, I thought, already developing someone whom others, yet unborn, will someday call "mother."

When The Gate Is Open

After graduating from Luther Seminary in 1960 I accepted a call to Trinity Lutheran Church in Fowler, Colorado. Fowler lay along the Arkansas River, about thirty miles east of Pueblo. To the south of town was "cedar and canyon" country, used exclusively for ranching. There were not many fences and one had to be careful driving at night because it was not unusual to encounter cattle on the highway. Even the paved roads had cattle guards. The ravines and creeks were dry most of the year but in the spring they could be raging torrents. There were stories of at least one person being swept away by an unexpected wall of water sweeping down the Apishapa, one of the little rivers that brought water from the mountains to the Arkansas River. Two Fowler folks who knew and loved this "Zane Gray" country took me to caves where the walls were decorated with old Indian drawings. One of the ranchers maintained a little cabin out there. In the best tradition of the West, it was never locked.

The locals referred to the higher country north of Fowler as the area of "dry land" farming. The fields were huge and the farmers planted the corn and wheat in such a manner as to trap maximum moisture. Local lore declared that when it rained the farmers drove

Cadillacs and when it didn't they drove Model As. One of the church families that lived twenty miles north of town had lost a six-year old boy to a rattlesnake bite.

The Arkansas River valley was from three to five miles wide. The farms in the valley were relatively small and were all irrigated. The farmers raised hay, tomatoes and sugar beets. Two large irrigation ditches that originated many miles west of Fowler brought water to the area from the Arkansas River. One was named the Otero and the other was called the Fowler ditch. Each of the ditches had a ditch rider. He not only maintained the ditch but also determined when the water would be released to each farmer. When it was a farmer's turn to receive water the ditch rider would call and tell him when he was going to open the gate. It was imperative that the farmer receiving the water be ready for it. Every other task had to be deferred. He might have to be out all night laying the tubes that were used to siphon off the water from one of his ditches into the fields. It was all done by gravitation.

It was not uncommon to have farmers in church on Sunday morning who had been out all night irrigating. At least that was the excuse they gave for nodding off during my sermons. Perhaps I was naïve, but I believed them! I had been a student for twenty years before going to Fowler, and I was impressed with the way the farmers worked. I had never sacrificed much "sack time" during my student days. Now I was surrounded by people making a living the old fashioned way. They earned it.

But all that hard work notwithstanding, it was the water released to each farmer that made all the difference in the world. When opened, the gates on the two big irrigation ditches provided a source for growth. They stood between agricultural success and failure. Though each farmer paid for his allotment, he would always think of the water as a gift—a gift of life.

There is a hymn in the *Lutheran Book of Worship* titled "Today Your Mercy Calls Us." I never sing that hymn but what I think of those irrigation ditches and the ditch rider opening the gates to let water flow to the farmers.

> "O all embracing Mercy, O ever open Door,
> What should we do without you When heart and eye run o'er?
> When all things seem against us, To drive us to despair,

We know one gate is open, One ear will hear our prayer." (#304)

A few years ago I saw a movie, based on a book by the same name, *"A River Runs Through It."* The mountain scenery was spectacular and the plot was fascinating, but it is the title itself that remains with me. It is a poignant description of life itself with the river of God's grace flowing through it. We are such gifted people, beginning with the gift of life and then moving through all those sustaining and exhilarating qualities that make up what we refer to as "our life." The heart that beats within us, the mind that explores the mysteries of God's creation, the senses that touch the texture of the world, see the emerging color of spring, smell the rain soaked forest on a fall day and hear the doleful call of the mourning dove, the muscles that stretch and strain to climb a hill—all are a gift from God to those whom He has made. And then there are the gifts of air to breathe, sunshine to warm the earth, rain to bring refreshment and the fertile soil to produce food and beauty. Beyond that we are gifted with the presence of other people who bring joy and meaning to life through our many relationships.

Perhaps the psalmist had all of that in mind and more when he wrote, "There is a river whose streams make glad the city of God." (*Psalm* 46: 4) The river to which the psalmist refers covers all the mercies of God experienced throughout the course of our life. We who live on this side of the resurrection of Jesus from the dead are keenly aware of the presence of the living Christ among us, bringing peace and the promise of forgiveness and eternal life to all who believe. We call this river "grace." Without it we would be dead.

The farmers in the Arkansas River valley had a reliable source of water that gushed through their gate at appointed times. The water flowed out through the gate and on to their fields through a network of smaller ditches and they directed it to those areas most in need of moisture. The opportunity to receive the water was one they took seriously and one to which they gave studied attention. It is not so different for us. While God's grace is a free gift and comes to us through the generosity of God, we need to be alert to the timing of grace and the need to apply it to those areas of our life where we are most withered.

Speaking Up

With a Father-Son banquet just around the corner at Trinity Lutheran Church in Fowler, Colorado, Jeter Arnold and I had the assignment of finding a suitable speaker. Jeter was a tall, strapping fellow who ranched south of town. He was also bright and insightful. He had heard of an Episcopalian priest from La Junta who was considered to be a good speaker, one who ought to appeal to a church basement full of men and boys.

So, at our earliest convenience, Jeter and I headed east to La Junta. We found the rectory and went up and knocked on the door. The priest's wife answered and told us her husband was gone but would be home soon. She asked if we would care to come in and wait. We decided to do just that. As we entered, a huge dog worked its way through the door and then followed us into the house. The priest's wife made us comfortable, serving cold drinks and engaging us in pleasant conversation. While we visited and enjoyed our beverages the dog romped through the house. One minute it was licking the baby's face, over the mild protests of the child's mother. The next minute the dog raced up the stairs. Our hostess told one of the older children to go get it and bring it back down. I thought to myself that she was overly permissive towards the dog. If it were my dog, I thought, I would have booted it out of the house and when the company was gone found a way to explain the facts of life to that hound. When the priest returned the dog continued its frolicking about the house. We quickly finished our business, said "good bye" and walked down the sidewalk towards our car. We were half way to our car when the priest opened the front door and called to us, "Hey, you forgot your dog!"

We explained to the couple that we had never seen that dog before. They told us they had never seen it before either. Each party thought it belonged to the other. But, what was most surprising to us was the patient suffering of the priest and his wife as they watched this unwelcome canine guest cruise the rectory. After we had all had our laughs over the absurdity of the situation, they both confessed to some private thoughts they had had during our visit which could be summed up as, "When are these rubes and their over-sized mongrel ever going to leave?" We told them we had thought they had a pretty undisciplined dog.

Are there times when it is better to speak up, to speak one's mind, than to remain silent and let private thoughts unravel into a pile of irritations? Some folks can do it so diplomatically that you hardly realize they are being confrontational. Something like, "Could you keep your dog beside you since our house really isn't very dog-proof," would have clarified the situation immediately. Suffering in silence may not always be the recommended solution to a relational problem.

On the other hand, there are those times when speaking one's mind may not be the most appropriate response. Many years ago, when our youngest son was about six or seven, I took him along with me to see a friend who owned a John Deere dealership in Watertown. My friend, Howard, saw that Erik was standing in front of the toys. It was obvious to both Howard and me that Erik wanted to leave with a toy tractor. Being a generous person, Howard walked over to the shelf and picked out a nice green John Deere tractor and presented it as a gift to Erik. We had taught Erik to say "thank you" whenever he was given something, and I expected our training to produce results that day. Instead, Erik responded by saying "I hate green."

Now if there is one thing you don't want to say in a John Deere establishment it is "I hate green." A string of cuss words might have been more bearable for a long time John Deere devotee than maligning the color green. What Erik meant was that he really preferred one of the yellow tractors that sat with the green ones on the shelf. He just lacked the verbal skills to express his preference gracefully. Howard gave him a yellow one. Now Erik had a new tractor and Howard had a good story. Would that all honest expressions of opinion had the same happy ending!

We usually criticize hypocrisy and praise honesty. But if we define hypocrisy as pretending to be, or to be thinking, something other than what we are, is that always wrong? And if we define honesty as being ourselves in all circumstances and saying exactly what we think, is that always right? Might there be times when it is more graceful and kind to be hypocritical and more ruthless and unkind to be honest?

It stretches our minds to consider those possibilities. And, if we are inclined to draw hard lines between right and wrong, black and white and good and bad, then we had better leave our value judgments about hypocrisy and honesty as they are. But, if we have some tolerance for a new thought, we can pursue the subject.

A child brings home a project from school. He is as proud as punch over the little piece of artwork that couldn't be botched more. By all standards, it is dreadful. But a thoughtful parent will praise the child for a job well done. That is graceful hypocrisy. A layman will stand up in church to read a lesson for the first time, overcoming a huge case of stage fright to do so. He doesn't project, he mispronounces words and he lacks expression. But a gracious pastor will seek him out after the service and tell him "good job." That is graceful hypocrisy. More often than not, when I have preached what I consider to be a poor sermon, I will encounter some kind person who tells me, "Thanks! I found that helpful." I know that person has chosen to be supportive rather than analytical as an act of kindness to me. I am grateful for this bit of graceful hypocrisy and encouraged to do better next time. There are times we feel miserable because of a sadness that has come to us. Someone asks us how it's going and, not wishing to project our misery on to another, we say "fine." Isn't that graceful hypocrisy? One could argue that, in every case, there has been a lack of honesty. But adhering to a principle may be less important than voluntarily yielding to another person.

Sometimes a little hypocrisy leads us in the right direction. We may, with great reluctance, go to a party or some other kind of social gathering. We don't want to be there but there just weren't any really good excuses. So we put on a little happy act. But, pretty soon, we overcome our feelings, find some good food or somebody interesting to talk to and before we know it we are enjoying ourselves. Our sense of civility and courtesy initially encouraged hypocrisy but eventually led to honest enjoyment. Sometimes hypocrisy is like stalling for time—time to get our act together.

Having said all this in praise of a selective hypocrisy, let me now say I believe there are also those times when we should not hide our feelings or thoughts but should be blatantly honest. Then, let the chips fall where they may.

Not long ago I watched the Minnesota Twins play the New York Yankees on television. Chuck Knoblauch, who had once played for the Twins, was now playing left field for the Yankees. He had come to the Yankees after expressing a desire to leave the Twins. Even though all of that had transpired four years earlier, there were still some Twins' fans harboring resentment over his rejection of his former team. A few of them in the left field bleachers threw whatever they could lay their hands on at Knoblauch. The umpires had to stop the game and call the Yankees off the field. The public address announcers pleaded for cooperation. The umpires threatened to make the Twins forfeit the game if the pelting of Knoblauch did not stop. Tom Kelly, the Twins' manager, walked out to left field in a most unusual gesture to try to get those "fans" who had probably tried to elevate their IQ with beer to stop their bombardment. Those engaging in that outrageous behavior were a very small percentage of the 40,000 fans at the game.

But, I wondered, what were all of those other legitimate fans doing when the hooligans were hurling the missiles? Why did they not either fetch the security folks or themselves tell the misfits to quit what they were doing? If there ever was a time for decent folks to stand up and be heard that was it. Maybe there was some honest, straight talk going on, but apparently not enough of it. Sometimes honesty takes almost more courage than we can muster.

Honesty is best when it is practiced for the benefit of others and not employed just as an excuse to unload our frustrations on others. Scripture tells us the tongue should be bridled in the interest of true religion. (*James* 1:26) To bridle the tongue does not mean to stop it, but to keep it under control. If thoughts about the appropriateness of selective hypocrisy and selective honesty help us control our tongues then these words may serve a purpose.

A Bugle?

Several years ago I hunted elk in the Black Hills. Bull elk call back and forth in the fall of the year as a part of the mating ritual. They are said to be "in rut" at the time. I had checked out some videos that gave practical advice on how to hunt the majestic animals. These videos provided instructions on how to reproduce the calls of both the bulls and the cows. The sound of the bull calling is referred to as a bugle. The cow's call has a strong resemblance to the "meow" of a house cat. I practiced both. The cow call was easy to reproduce. But the so-called bugle of the bull turned out to be a challenge. The sounds on the video, all I think recorded at a considerable distance from the bull, were clear and clarion-like, with multiple notes culminating in three grunts. My efforts, at best, sounded like the screams of the tormented rather than the clear, sweet tones of a bugle.

As it turned out, I wasn't that far off. On a clear and crisp morning, with sparkling stars overhead and the faint glow of the moon highlighting the meadows, I took a position at the base of a mountain to wait. I knew there were elk in the area because I had surprised several of the big animals into a noisy stampede the day before as I walked along a ridge. As the sky brightened in the east and I began to see and discern various objects, I blew softly on my cow call. A windless silence greeted my call. I waited. I called again. More silence.

And then the woods exploded with the bugle of a bull above me on a ridge, probably not more than seventy yards away. Did I say "bugle?" It sounded more like a defiant scream. And those concluding grunts could not have sounded more menacing. The instructional videos I had watched had suggested that, after hearing the first response, the hunter should try to move forward, cutting the distance between the bull and hunter in half. What they did not say was that every instinct in me towards self-preservation would have to be overcome in order to do that. I felt the alarm of someone who has been challenged to a duel. My first reaction was to get up and run, to double the distance between the elk and myself rather than cut it in half. My second thought, gaining some bravery, was to at least work my way behind a tree. I settled on staying put.

It became a standoff. I was too wary to move forward. The bull was not convinced that I was authentic and he held his ground. For thirty minutes we called back and forth. Eventually, after the woods fell silent, I gathered up enough courage to move up. By then he was gone. My timidity had cost me. On another day I would do better.

I have often thought of that wonderful morning. I keep coming back to my reaction to the initial call of the bull elk, euphemistically called a "bugle." In the absolute stillness of that Black Hills morning and as close as the bull was, his call sounded less like the clear and resonant melody of a bugle and more like an outcry or a shriek. It was startling. It was wild. It was beautiful.

Hearing the brazen and defiant "bugle" of the bull elk caused me to think of how we commonly use euphemisms in life in order to soften hard realities. We attempt to wrap hard truths in velvet and in the process cloud the truth. Not long ago I listened to someone who works in what we call "development," the raising of funds for institutions. He talked about a gift that would be coming at the time of a person's death. But, rather than use the "d" word, he said the gift would not be available until the person's "will matured." I thought that would make an interesting way to write an obituary: "Ole Olson's will matured yesterday afternoon at a local hospital." For that matter, we all try to soften that final reality (is that, too, a euphemism?). It is not uncommon among those who sell and buy life insurance to speak of that moment when or if "something should happen to you." The reference, of course, is to dying.

My wife has multiple sclerosis and is confined to a wheelchair. In an effort to keep pace with the most recent politically correct terms, people have referred to her condition as "physically challenged" or "differently abled." I think "physically handicapped" pretty much says it all and there is no need to try to soften the reality of her condition. I have passed sixty-five and I'm growing older by the day. Please don't refer to me as "chronologically advantaged." I played basketball with my granddaughters the other night and discovered I'd lost my hook shot, couldn't shoot my jump shot because there was no jump left in it and my dribbling was a pitiful and spastic spectacle. I felt "chronologically depleted" maybe, but mainly "old."

My all time favorite euphemistic phrase is one that appeared as the title of a little monograph about the Civil War shortly after the bitter conflict was over. It read: "An Unbiased Account of the Recent Unpleasantness Between the States from a Southern Point of View." To describe this national tragedy in which, according to Shelby Foote in his three volume Civil War narrative, a total of 623,026 North-South soldiers were killed and 471,427 were wounded, as a "recent unpleasantness" not only defies all logic but must have been bewildering to those who wore the blue and gray uniforms.

In his book, *Whatever Became of Sin?*, the famous psychiatrist, Dr. Karl Menninger, noted that the word "sin" had been a veritable watchword for the Biblical prophets. But now, he observed, it is a word that is rarely heard. He wondered if no one was any longer guilty of anything. Is the cause of our problems only that someone may have been stupid or sick or criminal—or asleep? Menninger's concern is more positive than it may seem. He is a healer. But healing cannot come without repentance or atonement, both of which begin with a consciousness of sin. We don't repent of weaknesses or slips. Nothing less than an awareness of disobedience towards God will do. Once that is acknowledged and we place ourselves at God's mercy we begin to fathom the generosity of God's love through the forgiveness of sins. Then we can accept ourselves, not because we have softened the nature of our behavior or tried to excuse it with euphemisms, but because we discover that God accepts us in spite of our rebellion, or unacceptable behavior.

Dr. Menninger quoted the American theologian, Paul Tillich, at length. Tillich had made the point that sin is the great, all-pervading problem of our life. To be in a state of sin (not just committing sins) is to be in a state of separation—from others, from ourselves and from God. Menninger added that separation is another word not only for sin, but for mental illness, for crime, for nonfunctioning, for aggression, for alienation and death. Thus the key to healing and growth lies in God's act of reconciliation through the cross and not in minimizing our condition. The separation gap can only be bridged from the other side, from God's side.

There is some value in saying what we mean and meaning what we say. Calling a spade a spade may be the most helpful in the long run. Euphemisms are usually intended to wrap velvet around a hammer and, in some instances, may be a graceful gesture. But when it comes to either facing or dodging the realities of life, we probably want to be as accurate as possible, even to the point of using a harsh word. If, on the other hand, it is only a matter of describing what a bull elk sounds like, it will do no harm to stick with the word, "bugle," euphemism though it may be.

Fear

I recall being afraid of two people when I was a kid, though the nature of my fear was different from person to person.

I feared Bob. He was a little older than I and a lot tougher. Moreover, he had a history of having a short fuse and winning some notable scraps. Bob had a brother, a little younger than I, with whom I once fought. I think maybe I came out ahead in that skirmish because he went home crying.

It had started as a domestic quarrel between Bob and his brother. I suppose I thought I might ingratiate myself to Bob by taking his side, which I did rather vigorously. But it turned out to be a serious miscalculation because blood was stronger than friendship and Bob resented my beating on his brother. For days I lived in fear of retaliation. Fortunately the reprisal never came, but the knot in my stomach remained for longer than I care to remember.

I was also afraid of my grandfather. But it was a different kind of fear altogether. I knew that nothing would ever cause him to lay a hand on me. I also knew that I was the apple of his eye, being the oldest grandson and regular summer companion in the hayfield. My grandfather was a powerful figure in my life. I had enormous respect for him. I appreciated the way he treated me and delighted in his approval. I was eager to avoid doing anything that would disappoint him. Even though it was he who drove me over to Dell Rapids from rural Garretson to buy my first suit, it was not the fear of his withholding material rewards that motivated my response. Rather, it was the fear of letting him down.

Fear is generally regarded as an undesirable emotion in adults. President Franklin Roosevelt reminded Americans "We have nothing to fear except fear itself." Fear can reduce us to helplessness and incompetence. It can cloud our thinking, stifle decisiveness and plunge us into panic. "Don't be afraid," we say, as we support one another in facing challenges.

But Scripture admonishes us to fear God. "For as the heavens are high above the earth," says the Psalmist in *Psalm* 103, "so great is his steadfast love toward those who fear him." What kind of fear is this? Is it like cholesterol? Is there good and bad fear?

Christian preachers used to deliver what we refer to as "hellfire and brimstone" sermons. The best known of these fiery preachers was the Puritan, Jonathan Edwards. His sermon, "Sinners in The Hands of an Angry God," became an event in American history. Edwards was not a bombastic shouter. He had a thin voice, spoke quietly and read his sermons. What made his sermons so powerful was the vivid imagery he used. God, proclaimed Edwards, "holds you over the pit of hell," much like one holding a spider or other loathsome insect over burning flames. God "abhors you and is dreadfully provoked," he warned. God's wrath "burns like fire." His listeners were ten thousand times more abominable in God's eyes than a snake was in theirs, Edwards charged. Jonathan Edwards attempted to scare hell out of his congregation by promoting a concept of a God seething with righteous anger. When his audience left the church they were afraid of God in much the same way I was afraid of my boyhood friend, Bob. They expected God to momentarily lower the boom.

The second form of fear, more akin to the kind of fear I had of my grandfather, was most clearly expressed by Martin Luther in the explanations he provided for the Ten Commandments in *Luther's Small Catechism*. He began each explanation of why we should keep the commandments with the phrase, "We should fear and love God. . ." It is interesting to note how Luther coupled fear with love as the emotional basis for obeying God's laws. Fear is now more like awe than fright. It is a fear of disrupting a very meaningful relationship, one that is anchored in respect. It is a fear of failing to please one to whom much is owed.

That is the kind of fear Jesus displayed throughout his life. The book of *Hebrews* declares, "In the days of his flesh, Jesus offered up prayers and supplications, with loud cries and tears, and he was heard for his godly fear." (*Hebrews* 5:7) The fear of God in the heart of Jesus was the fear of not being faithful and, therefore, not reflecting God's love and glory. It promoted within him a desire to be obedient.

I think it is evident that admonitions to fear God are not so much intended to produce a quavering heart as to encourage obedience. And, since obedience is not highly prized among adults, it may be worth further exploration. Of course we value obedience in children. A disobedient child is not a thing of beauty. Our reaction wavers between anger and bewilderment. But we don't focus on the subject of adult disobedience, especially towards God.

When I consider my life, which has been a mixture of obedience and disobedience, I think there are at least three conditions likely to foster obedience.

First, I tend to want to follow the rules when I understand the reason for the rule and it makes sense to me. I recall vividly a sordid record of disobedience towards my father in the matter of Sunday baseball games. As a pastor he was sensitive towards any kind of activity that detracted from church attendance, which he believed was the case with Sunday afternoon baseball games. But I loved baseball and was a loyal fan of the Oldham baseball team. They were good and fun to watch. And Joe Duffy, the manager, usually asked some of us boys to run down the foul balls during the game. I argued with my father that I should not be penalized because some of the players may have skipped church. After all, I hadn't! So after dad had said his final "no" I quietly slipped away from the house and went to the baseball park. His rule made no sense to me, and I didn't miss a game. Moreover, I think he knew it.

On the other hand, I meticulously observed dad's rules about handling a gun. It made sense to always assume the weapon was loaded, to avoid pointing it at anyone, to keep it clean and sequester it away from my younger brother. So my record of obedience was spotty and based on which rules were agreeable to me. My father must have wondered if a little military experience might not do me some good, where you obey the rules whether you like them or not. But he was patient and understood boys.

A second reason I tend to be obedient comes from knowing there is a stiff penalty attached to a violation of a law. I may not see any sense to the rule but, on the other hand, I don't want to suffer the consequences of disobedience. I may be absolutely convinced the limit of fish could be much higher, but I do not want to get caught with more fish than the law allows. I know that it might mean paying a fine, losing my fishing license and getting my name published in the court column. To gain the reputation of a game law violator is not a pleasant prospect, and so I keep a running count as the fish are reeled in and stop (fishing, not counting!) when the limit is reached.

The third reason I am obedient is when I trust those who make the rules. I may not understand the reason. I may not be intimidated by the consequences of breaking the rule. But I do trust the wisdom and judgment of the one who made it. Let's say that a modest load limit is posted on a country bridge. I am inclined to ignore the warning because I saw another vehicle of equal weight drive across it. It looks strong enough to me and there is no police officer in sight. But I decide to trust the judgment of the engineers who posted the limit. I will obey the law.

We are most likely to obey God's laws if all three conditions are present. So we really ought to try our best to understand why God has issued the commandments and placed the warnings in our consciences. What is there about them that suggest God has our best interests in mind? And we should carefully examine the possible consequences of our disobedience. When we break God's laws why is it that we are the ones, not the laws, which are broken? Perhaps they are more like an instruction manual for a new appliance, telling us what to do to make it work and what to avoid, so as not to break it. Finally, we should pray for the grace to trust the One who made the rules and simply obey them because we fear and love God above all things, much as I feared and loved my grandfather.

It's What You Know

My colleague in Watertown called on an elderly woman in one of the nursing homes of the city. She was a sweet woman who wanted to be helpful and carry her side of the conversation. She was in the not-so-early stages of dementia but managed through sheer charm to camouflage her limitations. My colleague, to make conversation, mentioned it was the four hundred fiftieth anniversary of the *Augsburg Confession,* the major doctrinal statement of the Lutheran Church. Later, I told him I thought he must have been desperate for something to talk about. But she thought for a while and then said in a surprised voice, "Has it been that long?" I suspect she might have said about the same thing if he had told her that it had been four hours since she had eaten lunch.

Her confusion notwithstanding, it was not an entirely inappropriate answer. It would be quite acceptable to wonder why Lutherans grant such stature to a document that old, issuing from a different country and culture and written in the context of a theological debate that is no longer so fervent. The *Augsburg Confession* was written in 1530 by one of the "brains" of the Protestant Reformation, Philip Melancthon, a friend of Martin Luther. Melancthon's purpose in writing it was to clarify the teachings of the Lutherans, especially as over against the Roman Catholic Church and other reformers, who in their "enthusiasm," the Lutherans believed, were taking the Protestant Reformation too far afield from historic Christianity. Today the *Augsburg Confession* remains at the center of the Lutheran confessional, or doctrinal, statements.

Other churches have similar documents, with historical footings, that continue to inform and shape their life and destiny. Given the greater understanding and cooperation between churches today it might be tempting to suggest the churches should scrap those unique documents that clarify the differences between them. Why not instead focus on all the beliefs they hold in common? But all of those historical statements are precious to each church. A more proper stance would be for each church to respect and acquaint itself with the unique perspective of the others. The dialogue would go something like this: "You tell us what you believe and we will tell you what we believe. Then we will celebrate our uniqueness, recognize how much we have in common and work and worship together."

Respecting what churches teach is important because otherwise Christianity slips into the mire of human feelings or becomes confused with "pop" culture and other half-baked notions than bear only a slight resemblance to Biblical truth. Each of us requires a faith based on what we know, rather than how we feel. Our churches help us achieve that.

In his novel, *Chesapeake*, James Michener describes the fortunes of the Paxmore family, a family of ship builders. In his usual style, he begins with the first generation of Paxmores and describes their fitful efforts at building a canoe out of a log. Then the Indians came to help. After hollowing out the log, they turned it over and drew a line down the center of the bottom. Then they scraped the wood away on either side, leaving a ridge, or backbone, down the center, thus forming a keel. When they floated the canoe the newly formed keel not only protected the bottom of the boat but also kept the boat from rocking and made it easier to hold a steady course in the wind.

In much the same manner our doctrinal statements perform the function of a keel on a boat. Amidst the shallows of much of modern thought our doctrines protect the integrity of the Faith. When the fickle winds of this or that fad blow strong and we are tempted to drift with the mood of the moment, our basic teachings help us to hold a steady course. And when the storms of life crash all around us we are not as likely to capsize emotionally if we can hold on to what we *know* to be true.

There are at least two poignant examples of how this works in the Old Testament. The first comes from the book of *I Kings* where we encounter Elijah, a prophet. He had just won a dramatic contest with the priests of the fertility god, Baal. He had demonstrated the futility of following a god who could not produce a miracle. It was a tremendous victory, and he celebrated it by having all four hundred fifty of the priests of Baal killed. You won't find many similarities to Mr. Rogers' neighborhood in the Old Testament! But Elijah goes into a kind of funk after that. Those prophets of Baal whom he had dispatched happened to be favorites of Queen Jezebel and she vowed to visit the same fate on him. So Elijah is forced to run and hide in a cave. He feels abandoned by God. As an answer to his complaint he is told by God to listen for His voice. But God is not to be heard in the wind or earthquake or fire, conditions that might seem favorable for a mighty God to utter a word. Instead, there came to him a voice in "a sound of sheer silence." "What are you doing here, Elijah?" said the voice. Elijah reiterated his sob story, detailing all of the reasons he felt sorry for himself. But the Lord would have none of that. There was nothing of the "I feel your pain" in the Lord's answer. Rather, the Lord told Elijah to get out of the cave, quit wallowing in his miseries and get to work. He gave him an assignment, which included finding his successor. He now had something solid to hang on to, something he knew, rather than what he felt. He could go with that.

The second Old Testament example is found in *Habakkuk*. Habakkuk lived and prophesied in a time of impending crisis. Foreign powers loomed on the horizon and the people around him were in a state of confusion and bewilderment. Habakkuk complains to God about his difficult assignment of keeping the faith, within himself and others. He concludes, "I will keep watch to see what he will say to me, and what he will answer concerning my complaint." The response comes quickly:

"Then the Lord answered me
and said:
Write the vision;
Make it plain on tablets,
So that a runner may read it." (Habakkuk 2:2)

Habakkuk is told to be patient: "If it seems to tarry, wait for it; it will surely come, it will not delay." The Lord lifts Habakkuk's sights to see a vision, one that will pull him out of himself and provide direction and inspiration for him. "The righteous live by their faith," God tells him. God reminds Habakkuk that faithfulness to the vision, the task, is what will carry the moment. Do the work, speak the message, and the conviction and joy will return in due time.

God called both Elijah and Habakkuk to live by what they knew to be true rather than be guided by how they felt at the moment. It is in response to this human need for objective truth that our churches teach the doctrines and lessons of our confessional statements and the scriptures. We are helped thereby to see life through God's eyes rather than ours, which are covered with glasses tinted by our emotional and psychological states. We do not deny the importance of feelings. On the contrary, they are a gift from the Creator. But we do acknowledge that they are a bit too whimsical and subject to varying moods to be the ultimate source for thought and action.

The English literary figure, Samuel Johnson, once wrote a quatrain not only to help us understand the difference between subjective and objective truth, but also to value the latter more.

"We've heard in language highly spiced
that Crowe does not believe in Christ,
but what we're more concerned to know
is whether Christ believes in Crowe."

We have our own moods and thoughts and they generally seem right to us, but depending on a variety of circumstances, they can be all over the place. They can also be pretty inconsistent. What carries the day, though, and provides a reliable beacon in the mists and vapors of uncertain human experience is God's Word. It reveals truth to us and that truth is clarified and focused by the teaching of our churches. Like the keel of a boat, our treasured Christian beliefs protect us and keep us balanced and steady in rough waters.

The Hand Shaker

Harold was not his real name, but everything else I tell you about him is true. Harold was rather shy and retiring, certainly not one to intrude himself into any gathering or to carry the conversation. Yet, he obviously liked being around other people. He seemed to be present at most gatherings, whether in church or in our home or the home of friends.

I remember one time in particular when he visited our home. He and my father stood chatting down in our basement. I had noticed that he shook hands with my father when he arrived. I also observed that during the course of his conversation with my father he shook dad's hand at least a couple of times. Then he prolonged his departure enough for two more handshakes with my father.

When Harold left I asked my father about Harold's hand shaking habit. Dad smiled and acknowledged that Harold seemed to enjoy, even require, the ritual as some kind of assurance that things were going well. It was sort of like making sure you were on the same page with him.

But that was fifty years ago and I had forgotten the incident. So it was startling, several years ago, when I returned to Oldham and ran into Harold. He did not look much older to me then than he had looked when I was a kid watching him and dad visit. We shook hands. Then, when he realized who I was—that is, whose son I was—he grabbed my hand again. As we talked he seized my hand at least once more. Then, in parting, we shook hands again—twice. All of the handshakes were done with conviction. Harold put a lot of himself into each one.

I thought at the time that I should arrange for a meeting between Harold and one of my children, just to carry on a family tradition. It would be a small way for them to be in touch with their grandfather, who shook the same hand.

Since then I have heard some disturbing news. Harold had retired to Oldham and ate his meals at the only café in town. When he entered the café he made it a ritual to go around and shake everybody's hand. During the town's centennial celebration many natives returned and they, too, looked to the café as a source of nourishment. But they were not as patiently disposed towards Harold's habit as the regulars. When they had washed their hands before eating they were not so eager to clasp the hand of a gentleman whom they had not seen in decades. Some complained. So the proprietor had to intervene and try to talk Harold out of an act of pure friendliness. It proved to be more difficult than he had expected. Old, familiar habits are not broken so easily. Harold had not changed, but the world around him had.

We now live in a world where touching is suspect. Those who are concerned with the spread of germs fear contamination. Those who fear sexual motivation recoil from any kind of touching, especially a man touching a child, even if it does not come close to what we would define as "inappropriate." For that matter, if I happen to be out walking and encounter children I don't know, I am almost fearful of speaking to them. All of these fears are grounded in some story or event, but the challenge comes in keeping it all in balance, and not being absolutely silly about it.

It is my conviction that touching is good and can be very meaningful. When I pray with a person, especially in the hospital, I will often take his or her hand. And if the person is semi-conscious I will often place my hand on his or her brow, to give a benediction. In those situations touching may be more than an act of friendliness; it may convey an energy and contribute to the healing process in some mysterious way. I am not at all surprised to see a football team hold hands in the huddle. The act itself has a binding quality much stronger than if each should say to the other, "we're together."

Dr. Paul Brand and Philip Yancey teamed up to write a book called *Fearfully and Wonderfully Made*. The subtitle reads, "A Surgeon Looks at the Human and Spiritual Body." In the chapter called "Skin" the authors talk about the role of tactile stimulation during and especially following birth. They describe how as late as 1920, the death rate among infants in some foundling hospitals in America approached 100 percent. Then Dr. Fritz Talbot of Boston brought from Germany an unscientific-sounding concept of "tender loving care." While visiting the Children's Clinic in Dusseldorf, he had noticed an old woman wandering through the hospital, always balancing a sickly baby on her hip. She was identified as "Old Anna." Hospital workers explained how after they had done everything they could do medically, and the babies were still not doing well, they turned the babies over to "Old Anna." She would cure them.

American institutions were initially reluctant to accept the concept that simple touching could improve their care. Statistics, however, soon convinced them. When Bellevue Hospital in New York established a rule that all babies should be picked up, carried around and otherwise "mothered" several times a day, the infant mortality rate dropped from 35 percent to less than 10 percent.

In *The Acts of the Apostles*, the New Testament book that describes the history of the early church, the apostles discovered they needed to find persons to help them with the many practical matters demanding their attention. "It is not right," they said, "that we should neglect the word of God in order to wait on tables." So they asked the community to select seven men of good standing. Then, as these chosen men stood before them, the apostles prayed and laid their hands on them, conscious of being empowered by the Holy Spirit, who created and sustained the church. Somehow the Spirit would energize and equip these seven men through prayer and the "hands on" blessing of the apostles.

The practice of the laying on of hands has continued in the Christian Church. It is a part of the ordaining of clergy in many denominations. A few denominations have invested the practice with the assurance of continuity from the early apostles. The doctrine is called "Apostolic Succession," referring to the actual succession of laid on hands all the way back to the apostles. Other Christians believe an adherence to the faith of the apostles is the more appropriate form of "succession." In either case, there is Biblical precedent for the placing of hands upon those who are entering a religious vocation. A special blessing is bestowed through one person touching another in God's name.

In a less formal way, we all understand the importance of touching one another. Friendship, love and compassion are all spiritual realities. But to make these concepts real we often rely on various physical expressions, such as hugs, kisses, embraces, handshakes and pats. That seems to be the way we are built, for whatever reason.

If in heaven, we are less in need of all these concrete symbols of spiritual realities we will have less touching. If not, I would venture Harold, who died not long ago, has made the rounds of heaven several times, offering his hand, more than once, to whomever will take it.

Jello

Our family's version of "eating out" in Oldham in the 1940s was quite different from today's practice of selecting among a variety of fast and slow food places that seem to be multiplying in most communities. Eating out for us—a pastor's family—usually meant going over to the church after school and catching the tail end of a post funeral meal. I never minded that because the food was pretty good and the choices were challenging. One could savor a sampling from several kinds of hot dishes, though tuna casseroles always seemed to be on the verge of taking over. Jello was a given, of course. But there were enough flavors of jello to further the illusion of variety. It came in at least four colors: red, yellow, orange or green, with corresponding flavors. Most of the jello dishes contained sliced bananas. A few included shavings of cabbage. Some were topped with whipped cream. My favorite was orange jello with chopped cabbage and whipped cream.

Often there were sandwiches, usually of the ham salad variety. Sometimes they were made with homemade buns and then it was hard to stop with just two. The real challenge came in picking the right piece of cake. That choice often involved a compromise because it did not often happen that the right frosting was on the right cake. But if I could find a piece of yellow cake with chocolate frosting the selection came as easy to me as crowing to a rooster.

Twice a year, eating at the church revolved around a celebration. On Easter Sunday, after the Sunrise Service, we gathered for a hearty breakfast of bacon, fried eggs and toast. I think my personal record was six eggs, a modest feat compared to the ravages of a couple of my friends from the farm. The other notable exception to the jello and hot dish menu was the New Year's Eve Watch Night Service oyster stew feed. When mother made oyster stew at home the oysters were carefully rationed and the milk did not seem creamy. But when the farm women made oyster stew at the church they served up bowls of rich, buttery milk, teeming with oysters. It was a solemn declaration of war on all arteries. This was, after all, the pre-cholesterol era of civilization. But what a way to bring in the new year!

I believe it was Mahatma Gandhi, the Indian liberator, who said that sometimes God must come first to people through a loaf of bread. I sometimes think God came to me first through a bowl of jello. If not God, certainly Lutheranism did.

There is a story in the New Testament where God came to people through bread. The story of Jesus feeding five thousand people with five barley loaves and two fish is found in *Mark* 6. When Andrew, one of the disciples of Jesus, reported the meager resources he had located he sensibly concluded with a disclaimer, "but what is that among so many?" As it turned out, it was enough to feed the tired and hungry pilgrims who had been more occupied with their spiritual hunger than their physical needs.

Is the task facing God any easier today? Seventy per cent of the earth is covered with salt water. Of the land that remains about one third is forest and one seventh is desert. Further, subtract all of the land covered by fresh water lakes, cities, roads, parking lots and various other developments. Probably less that fifteen per cent of the earth's surface is capable of agricultural production. And a fraction of that is disabled each year by drought, hail and floods.

When God made us and told us to multiply He assumed the responsibility of feeding us. Given the relative scarcity of tillable acres we are likely to say to God, as Andrew did to Jesus, "What is that among so many?" What God has managed to do is nothing short of a miracle and each time we take a summer drive into the country, viewing the grain and corn fields and the pastures with cattle, we are witnesses to this miracle. That some of the human population is starving does not mean that God has come up short in providing food. Rather, it means that humans have failed in its distribution.

So the miracle that Jesus accomplished as he fed those five thousand folks who had thoughtlessly left home without a sack lunch is about the same kind of miracle God performs every day. But there is more meaning to Jesus' miracle beyond providing a lesson about God's feeding of the world.

Every miracle Jesus performed was really an acted out parable. Each miracle was meant to teach a spiritual truth as well as to be a response to an immediate need. Those people who sat down on the grass to eat their fill found a greater fulfillment than the loaves and fish offered. "Do not work," Jesus admonished, "for the food that perishes, but for the food that endures for eternal life, which the Son of Man will give you." Later Jesus reveals the source of this enduring bread. "I am the bread of life," he says.

God comes to us through bread. When Jesus told his disciples to pray for "daily bread" in the Lord's Prayer we believe he had both kinds of bread in mind. He meant the kind of bread that comes in a loaf, made from the grains of the earth. This bread is a sign of God's power and care for his people. It is a major miracle that there is bread enough for all. And when it is given to one who is hungry it becomes the first signal that God blesses us. Sometimes it is not possible to impress people with the old story of God's love until they have tasted this gift that sticks to the stomach.

And then there is the bread of life, which comes to us in the person of Jesus. It satisfies the hungering of the human spirit. It gives rise to hope. It creates and sustains faith. It encourages love. It sticks to our hearts, because Jesus stays with us.

The noted missionary pastor, D.T. Niles, once said, "Evangelism is one beggar telling another beggar where to get a piece of bread." Or, as the case may be, a bowl of jello.

On Track

If being "in a rut" is anything like being "on track" it deserves a better rap than it has received. Going where someone else has first gone, if it is the best way, may be the only sensible approach in any kind of journey. If we take a detour now and then or go beyond the former destination, it does not detract from our indebtedness to those who pioneered. Most of us have experienced those "ah ha" moments in life when we suddenly realize how beholden we are to those who have gone before us and what a wonderful job they did in preparing the way for us.

Such was my state of mind as we biked our way through the Black Hills, from north to south, on the George S. Mickelson Trail. The Trail was once a railroad, constructed in 1890 as a trunk line of the Burlington Railroad. It began in Edgemont and ended in Deadwood. Two railroads had been in fierce competition to be the first to reach Deadwood and thus capitalize on the booming gold mining economy. The other line approached Deadwood from the east, a much easier task than to run a line lengthwise, south to north, through the heart of the Black Hills. In spite of the challenges facing the Burlington line, it won the race to Deadwood.

I suppose if we were asked to list the major engineering feats in the Black Hills we would put the great stone carvings, Mt. Rushmore and Crazy Horse, at the top. Then we might add a couple of caves, Pactola and Angostura dams, the Needles Highway and a bridge or two. Few of us would think of the railroads. But it is my conviction, after our trail ride, that the building of a railroad through the Black Hills is as impressive an accomplishment as any of the above. Railroad tracks are not like the highways, which pretty much go up and down as the hills and valleys dictate. Instead, there are long stretches (up to twenty miles) of steady inclines and declines, with no more than a four per cent grade. The work of the surveyors was crucial in finding a path which would be reasonably level. Then engineers had to design bridges, tunnels, trestles and mountain cuts, all of which were built by workers using horses. Sometimes they went around the back side of the mountain. Often they stayed close to the creeks. Their task was to make it gradual.

As a biker I felt a bit like an interloper. Those who built the railroad had no idea that some day it would be used as a bike path. Had they known, they might have put down their shovels and put the horses out to pasture. The modern concept of recreation was probably a foreign one to them. Build a peddler's path? Forget it.

With plenty of time to think, I pondered how this bike trek through the Hills was much like life itself. We are all indebted to those who have gone before us who have laid out tracks upon which we travel. We grow up in communities built by others. We live under a great government created and established by others. We thrive under the freedoms guaranteed to all Americans, secured and defended at great cost by others. We inherit a wealth of art, literature and music the day we are born into the world. Our material benefits have come from the ingenuity and hard work of others. Prior advances in science and technology are now our legacy. I'm reminded of the admonition to be modest because a lot was accomplished before we were born.

The psalmist carries this sense of indebtedness even farther: "The Lord is my chosen portion and my cup; you hold my lot. The boundary lines have fallen for me in pleasant places; I have a goodly heritage." (*Psalm* 16: 5,6)

I love that passage. With its mixture of privilege and gratitude it expresses what so many of us feel. We are glad to be who we are and where we are. And we recognize that we had relatively little to do with either. Grandparents, parents and other adult role models pretty much built the tracks upon which we now travel. That would be especially true with our faith journey. I worship the same God, sing the same hymns, pray the same prayers, follow the same Lord and serve him in much the same way as my fathers and mothers in faith did. Some day, in the phraseology of the Old Testament, I shall be gathered to them and their God.

In her novel, *O Pioneers!*, Willa Cather described the melancholy of Alexandra who recalled her father and mother and others who were gone, many of them old neighbors. What had once been wild prairie was now a graveyard. Now that the generation ahead of her was gone and she had grown old, she had the sense of being in the front line. Carl responds to her whimsical thoughts. "And now the old story has begun to write itself over there," said Carl softly. "Isn't it queer: there are only two or three human stories, and they go on repeating themselves as fiercely as if they had never happened before; like the larks in this country, that have been singing the same five notes over for thousands of years."

The writer of *Ecclesiastes*, a part of the Wisdom Literature of the Old Testament, reflected, too, on the apparent repetition of life.

> "What has been is what will be,
>   and what has been done is
>   what will be done;
>   there is nothing new under
>   the sun.
> Is there a thing of which it is said,
>   'See, this is new?'
> It has already been,
>   in the ages before us." (*Ecclesiastes* 1:9,10)

At the very least, as we consider the impact on us of the generations before us, it might be well to acknowledge the strong connection between the then and now. Many of our congregations have gone to two types of worship services, calling one the traditional and the other contemporary (or some variation thereof). Perhaps those terms are best because we all understand the difference between the two. But this distinction is unfortunate if it conveys the notion that traditions have no contemporary value or that anything called contemporary is not heavily endowed with past traditions. In truth, there is only a very subtle difference between the two, more in style than in content. The past is and always will be very much with us.

Riding on the Mickelson trail caused me to feel a heavy indebtedness to those who had preceded me—not only to those who had built the original railroad track, I might add, but also to those who had worked to make it into a bike trail. It caused me to reflect on the impact of one generation on another in the ongoing saga of life. It gave me pause to think of how beholden I was to those who prepared the road of life on which I now travel. And, beyond that, it caused me to think of what I was doing to lay out a good trail for those who follow me.

Out West

Certain words do something special for us. They stir our imaginations. Like good poetry, they evoke pleasant feelings and prompt us to probe deeper into our thoughts. Words, after all, are symbols. The communicator encodes his thoughts into the most fitting word-symbol and then puts it into writing or the spoken word. It is then transmitted to the printed page or flies through the airways to the intended recipient who must then decode it. If the decoder is on roughly the same page as the encoder the meanings will be transmitted quite accurately. However, it is possible the word-symbol may evoke more or less meaning to the reader or hearer than the sender intended.

I think that may be the case with the word "west" for me. I find it to be a word loaded with heavy and wonderful freight. Our English language is a remarkable treasure, but we rarely take time to savor it. Not many years ago the concept of speed-reading was highly promoted. The idea was to scan the page as quickly as one could and then retain more and more as one developed the skill. I suppose it has its place, but I prefer to go a little slower and taste the words. I gain as much, if not more, pleasure in how the author uses words as I do in absorbing the content, particularly now that I am out of school and not going to be tested on the material! For example, though my interest in various spectator sports has diminished over the years, I continue to read *Sports Illustrated* because of the high quality of the writing.

Maybe my fascination with the word "west" began when I was very young. Our home was on the west side of Oldham, adjacent to Case's field, with the horizon a mile or so beyond. One of our kitchen windows faced west and my mother often expressed her delight in seeing the gorgeous South Dakota sunsets. Our kitchen was all white so that when the late afternoon sun shone on the wall opposite the window the square of colors stood out like a Rembrandt painting. Various shades of yellow, red, orange and purple would gradually slide across the wall as the sun descended in its diagonal course. Even on the coldest of winter days the beams of sunlight brought a golden glow into the entire room, creating a warmth unrelated to the temperature.

My folks did not allow me to go to movies when I was young. At the time I thought that was the height of deprivation. I satisfied my need for stories either by reading comic books or listening to the radio, both of which engage one's imagination more than looking at pictures I think. Another result of the theater ban was that I never saw the *Wizard of Oz* until I was an adult when it was shown on television. The only benefit I can see from my delayed exposure to that classic is that the Wicked Witch of the West never had a chance to tarnish the word "west" for me. Had I sat as a little kid, cringing under the evil spell of the witch in our tiny theater in Oldham, "west" may have taken on more sinister shades of meaning.

I belong to the generation that grew up watching some pretty good westerns on television. I'm not sure they packed the punch of the Lone Ranger on radio, but such programs as *Gun Smoke, Have Gun Will Travel* and *High Chaparral* held my interest for many years. They were all sort of white hat verses black hat approaches to life on the frontier. In spite of their simplicity, or maybe because of it, many of us found these westerns with their predictable outcomes to be wonderful viewing. It is cleansing to get involved with a story where, even though evil comes on strong at the beginning, good eventually prevails. John Wayne took this western morality theme to its greatest heights in the movies. So, once again, the word "west" took on a unique charm as all of these stories unfolded in the canyon and cedar country to the west of all of us. It was nice to know that law and order was being established out in that country that was so beautiful but seemed to have more than its share of outlaws.

"West" has been a word that has struck hope into the hearts of many Americans. When Horace Greeley, the New York newspaperman, issued the advice in 1837, "Go West young man, go forth into the Country," he encouraged youth to escape the poverty and unemployment in the East. Whether it was the prospect of free land, gold or fewer restrictions, many Americans have headed towards the setting sun with great hope in their breasts. They were often lured onward by various promoters who themselves would profit from added numbers. Some who came to the western frontier after they had been told it was the "garden spot" of the world eventually turned their wagons around and headed back east, hanging signs on their wagons that read, "In God We Trusted, In Kansas We Busted." But for those not afraid of work, who could make their own luck, the western frontier was a place of opportunity and fulfilled hopes. "West" took on the meaning of a new start.

South Dakota is one of those states ranging from north to south where the West truly begins. Cross the Missouri River and you are there for sure. Maybe it comes a little sooner here and there. Tourists are often unprepared for the change in landscape. They gradually begin to realize they are seeing both more and less--more land and sky and less of what we think of as civilization. Those who know the book *Alice In Wonderland* may recall the King's words to Alice: "Isn't it marvelous—to see nothing and at such a great distance." Some regard the trip from the Missouri River to the Black Hills as an ordeal to endure. The High Plains holds no allure for them. They regard it as boring.

But there is more to the High Plains West than most of those who hasten through it imagine. Try camping overnight on some high ground. When you have extinguished the lantern, step out into the darkness and have a look above and around. All you see is sky, big sky. Stars shoot across the sky, lightning flashes miles and miles away, with no thunder or rain to show for it, and the wind blows lightly across the short grass prairie, with nothing at all to slow it down. You will feel small, even insignificant. It is a humbling and unforgettable moment and a good time to strike up a conversation about deeper things with your companions. You're apt to recall the words of *Psalm* 8:

> "When I look at your heavens,
>> the work of your
>> fingers,
> the moon and the stars
>> that you have established:
> what are human beings that
>> you are mindful of
>> them,
> mortals that you care for them?" (*Psalm* 8:3,4)

In the course of various kinds of hunting I have seen some ruggedly beautiful scenery out in that country that looks so flat and uninteresting to the impatient traveler. One of my favorite spots is in Harding County, where they don't even bother to put up fences between North and South Dakota. On one of our last trips out there all of us took our antelope in the morning, so our rancher host suggested that we take a ride in the afternoon. We had three All Terrain Vehicles at our disposal. We followed the rancher, and within a mile of the ranch we were in country rivaling the Badlands. In fact our friend and host, Alfred, refers to this part of his ranch as "the badlands." It, too, looked like "hell, with the fires burned out," a description General Custer applied to the better-known Badlands 200 miles to the south. We followed Alfred down hills and into gullies we never would have tackled on our own. In due time we were examining the partially exposed remains of a dinosaur. Some expert would be coming out to see if it was salvageable, Alfred said. We kept going and soon we were finding prime examples of petrified wood. That seemed odd in that there were no trees around there now. I thought the usual phrase, "well, times have changed," would be fairly inadequate to explain the change from lots of trees to no trees. Then we wound our way deeper into the heart of the country. We parked our ATVs and followed Alfred thirty feet up a sharp embankment. He pointed to a number of bones protruding out of the clay. "Petrified buffalo bones," he explained. This had once, many hundreds of years ago (long before the Sioux Indians came on the scene), been the site of a buffalo kill. Erosion had lowered both the top of the hill and the gully below so that now the bones were half way up the bank.

It is astonishing to think of what we saw that day, to think of how we stood in the presence of things that had been alive thousands of years ago. Our earth has a grand and glorious history and it tells its story in little ways here and there in remote places. It seems absurd that anyone could come charging into life acting as though he owned the place. We have our time here and then slip inexorably into the majestic history of the earth, "earth to earth, ashes to ashes, dust to dust."

So the West is for me a place of beauty, adventure and instruction. Turn me loose and I will head west. If I'm ever jailed and manage to escape I'll make it easy for my pursuers; I'll run west. I can't honestly support this preference for the West from sacred scripture.

But I do find it interesting to note what happened to Adam and Eve after they had disobeyed God in the Garden of Eden. When God punished them by driving them out of the Garden, he drove them east of Eden. Not only did God deprive them of the Garden, he made them go east! In my opinion, sending them west would not have been much of a penalty. In fact, it would have almost been a reward for disobedience. Such is the power of my prejudice. Go figure.

Representatives

Augustana Academy used to be a Lutheran high school in Canton, South Dakota. It closed its doors to students in the early 1970s for financial reasons. When I was a student there, back in the early 50s, we were often reminded that, whenever we left the campus, we were representing the school. In fact, we were told that we embodied the school. People who would never set foot on the campus or who would never meet anyone else from the school would form their opinion of the place based on our example. We carried the warning with us that bad behavior by us would result in someone forming a negative image of the Academy. On the other hand, our good behavior would reflect positively on the entire institution. So whether we ventured forth as members of the choir or athletic and forensic teams or made a solo visit to our homes we were always aware of a certain obligation to throw the best light possible on our school. Ideally, each of us was to be a personification of Augustana Academy. We weren't expected to always win the game or sing or speak well, but we were asked to remember our point of origin.

I never felt that was unfair. One could argue that we weren't free to be ourselves. After all we were being asked to be something other than ourselves, namely Augustana Academy. But I think most of us considered it an honor to be representatives of the school, and we embraced the idea. We liked the Academy well enough to want it to have a good reputation. We were personally expanded by this assignment and accepted the responsibility as a fair exchange for the loss of some of our personal freedom.

Ray Bradbury, in his science fiction novel, *Fahrenheit 451*, wraps the plot around the character of Montag, a fireman. As a fireman, Montag is expected to redirect his efforts to starting rather than extinguishing fires. Building materials have ceased to be flammable so firemen are not needed for their traditional service anymore. Specifically the firemen are now engaged in burning books, which will ignite at 451 degrees Fahrenheit. The power brokers of society consider books to be treacherous and so they set out to eradicate them. Books have become a threat to TV, which has become all-consuming. For example, Montag's wife spends her aimless and empty days watching TV, which covers three walls of one room. She is hoping to make the fourth wall into a TV screen too. Science has made it possible for her to receive the scripts of the programs and to interact with the TV soaps. She is totally absorbed by all of this and wholly unfulfilled.

In response to this fascist plot by the authorities a resistance movement, dedicated to preserving books, is formed. Because everyone has a photographic memory and total recall, each member of the literary underground has the ability to memorize entire books.

When their revolution has succeeded they will then recall the book and put it back into print once again. In the meantime they assume the identity of the author and the book they have committed to memory. One of them is known as Plato's *Republic*, another is Jonathan Swift's *Gulliver's Travels*. They go by the names of Thomas Jefferson, Abraham Lincoln and Albert Schweitzer. Matthew, Mark, Luke and John are there too. They regard themselves as being little more than dust jackets, of no significance personally compared to the wisdom they enshroud. They have become what they represent. They have let their personal identity become immersed in a greater identity.

A few years back we celebrated the golden anniversary of Mt. Rushmore, the great mountain carving in the Black Hills. Speakers reminded us that each of the four presidents carved in rock represented great American achievements. George Washington symbolized independence and the birth of a nation. Thomas Jefferson symbolized a vision of democracy and national expansion. Abraham Lincoln symbolized human equality and national unity. Theodore Roosevelt symbolized political reform and conservation of America's vast and beautiful natural resources. Each of the huge faces on the mountain represents more than the individual man.

In that same sense, though on a lesser scale, each person represents some idea, some cause, some commitment for good or for bad. Each of us is a walking, talking, breathing symbol of something beyond ourselves. We are even if we stand for nothing, for that, too, says something. We cannot escape being representatives.

This is especially true whenever we raise a flag of membership over our heads. When we join any kind of a group, but especially a church, we assume the obligation of being a representative. From that day on there will be folks who evaluate the group or organization that we have joined by observing us. Often, in our eagerness to discover what membership can do for us, we forget to explore the options of what we can do for the organization and what it will mean to now be identified as a member. This business of being a member is really a staggering obligation. Membership calls us to be representatives, that is to re-present to others the meaning of that to which we belong.

Each word we speak is a symbol of a meaning beyond it. Certain motions we make are forms of body language, saying more than we know. Each commitment we undertake is a symbol of the values we espouse. We are all pointers to something beyond ourselves. We are living signs.

The apostle Paul lifted this truth to a new level. He referred to himself, and by implication other believers, when he used the term "ambassador." He was, he said, an ambassador for Christ. It's a term borrowed from political circles where an ambassador represents one country to another country. He lives away from home and interprets the actions and expectations of his country to another. He is not expected to spout his own opinions. His role is to represent his country, in his words and actions. Then he relays the concerns and hopes of the people among whom he lives back to his own country. An ambassador is a go between, like a priest who brings God to the people and the peoples' concerns to God. And so it is quite something to say we believe in the priesthood of all believers. It means we are ready to accept the role of being a representative for God.

"C. B."

If any dentist could have, or would have, pulled each tooth with one yank and all of them in one sitting it would have been the late C.B. Wiles of Watertown. C.B. was a big, strong man and a genuine character. He was a little rough around the edges with a gargantuan sense of humor. He never chuckled; he roared. My last encounter with "C.B." took place on the sidewalk of downtown Watertown. He pulled out of his pocket a plastic bag full of jerky and gave me a nine-inch strip. Then he bellowed out an earthy story, one he may have saved for the Reverend. He found great delight in the humor of the story and in the fact that he was having a shot at shocking the pastor.

But with "C.B." all you had to do was go the distance. After the initial bombast and bluster the real "C.B." began to emerge. Soon we were past the raucous stuff and on to more serious topics. As we parted he recited some poetry that was clearly dear to him. He had no idea who wrote it; I later discovered it was Emily Dickinson. In that unlikely spot, in downtown Watertown, "C.B." delivered a poetic rendition from memory that might have won him first place in an oral interpretation event. He said:

"I never saw the moor,
I never saw the sea,
Yet know I how the heather looks,
And what a wave must be.

I never talked with God,
Nor visited in heaven,
Yet certain am I of the spot,
As though a chart were given."

C. B. might approach a patient in the dental chair as though he were going to excavate a mammoth site, but "forget" to send a bill to someone who had fallen on hard times. He was a diamond in the rough. He was also a man of faith. True, in choir practice in his Congregational church, he could produce twitters by writing and circulating suggestive doggerel. But, more to the point, he was there in the choir whooping his praises through his deep tones in the rich verses of an anthem, a medium his robust soul required.

We know the truth of the maxim, "Don't judge a book by its cover," but often find it hard to put it into practice. Failure to heed this counsel may be more prevalent in religion than anywhere else. We often confuse a passive personality with a religious one. A melancholy or aggressive temperament strikes us as irreligious. But it is doubtful whether any one type of personality, or all the variations in between, is any indication of faith, or the lack of it.

Certain branches of psychology have made much of human temperaments, drawing from sources as far back as Hippocrates in ancient Greece. They have identified four distinct types of personalities. Each type is determined by the glands of internal secretion, such as thyroid, pituitary, adrenals, parathyroid and the islands of Langerhans. Given the fact that temperament is controlled by body fluids, it is pretty much out of our control as to what type of personality we will have. Advocates of this theory readily concede that all humans possess a mixture of each of these types, thus reducing the theory of some of its force.

Of the four, the most desirable type of temperament is the sanguine. This is a happy and well-balanced person whose emotions are appropriate to the situation. This person cries when that is a fitting response and laughs when that is proper, taking the ups and downs of life in stride.

From the easy going and pleasant sanguine temperament we begin the downhill slide to the choleric personality. This is a forceful and aggressive person, constantly needing to prove his or her own power to one's self and to others. The choleric temperament radiates tension and makes others tense as well.

The melancholic type is a brooding individual who dwells on past mistakes and fears trying anything new lest more mistakes be made. Doubt and caution prevail. The melancholic person is likely to dwell on himself and thus is unable to allow thoughts of others or contact with others to take up valuable time he needs to focus on himself.

Sinking to the bottom of the scale we encounter the phlegmatic temperament. This person stands almost outside of life and connects to the normal style of living infrequently. The phlegmatic personality can best be described as a sick personality. Alfred Adler, in his book, *Understanding Human Nature*, calls such a person a "stranger to life."

However much we may buy into this old theory of human personality we must admit that one's temperament, whether determined by birth (including, maybe, the activity of our glands) or conditioned by environment, is a given in life. To some extent one's personality may be altered by therapy, drugs, self help practices, prayer and the love of others. But there is probably a static element that will always be with us and provide at least some definition of who we are.

Having said all of that, what we must remember is that any type of personality is capable of faith in God, even a deep and unshakeable faith. It is just that the personality traits that conform to our version of piety, such as being loving, peaceful and joyous, may not always be evident in equal measure from one person to another. The faith may be there but the temperamental machinery for manifesting it may be varied, or even deficient.

Is it possible that Jesus had that in mind when he cautioned people not to judge one another, lest they too be judged? Only God sees the heart. Only God truly knows what kind of human nature we have inherited and what has gone into making us what we are.

The measurements we apply to people are really quite inadequate and therefore the conclusions we draw may be inappropriate. I have a friend who has traveled widely throughout South Dakota. He has eaten in many establishments in a variety of towns. He has concocted what I call "Raymond's Law." It goes like this: "The smaller the town, the larger the pancake." That may be true, generally speaking, but I have been served gigantic pancakes in large towns and I suspect there must be some small town establishments where they have discovered that to turn over a profit they have to keep the pancakes small.

At any rate, when it comes to measuring people (as we all do, whether we should or not) there are no tidy categories. It's best, maybe, just to take people as they are, to put the best interpretation on what they say and do, to be sure that God can figure out a way to speak to them and live within them and not to demand that everybody express those deep meanings and beliefs in the same way. Just as the apostle Paul talked about a variety of spiritual gifts given to believers, so we may want to allow for a variety of expressions of the Christian faith.

In all honesty, C.B. Wiles would not have been on my list as a potential speaker for the mayor's prayer breakfast. The thought of that causes me to smile. He certainly would have made us forget the cold toast! There would have been some moments of uneasiness and wondering if we could risk laughing as robustly as we wanted. He would have had some salty things to say about life in God's world. After all, didn't Jesus say we were to be the "salt of the earth?" And maybe it would not be inappropriate to describe God in more earthy terms than we normally use. God did come to this earth to live among us, as one of us. God does come now to us through those earthly elements of water, bread and wine. It's always a good thing, I think, to release Jesus from the stained glass windows and let him walk with us, just as he walked with the needy on the dusty roads of Galilee.

Jake's Words

I had just returned home from a three-day turkey hunt in the Black Hills when the telephone rang. It was our daughter Kari calling and of course that meant a brief visit with grandson Jake came as a bonus. Jake was three years old at the time. I told him how I had been hunting turkeys and how much fun I'd had and that someday he would have to come along with me. Of course he asked if I had shot a turkey. I had to tell him that no, grandpa did not get a turkey this year. "But grandpa," he said, "if you want to get a turkey you have to go into the forest."

Never mind that I had just spent three exhausting days in the Black Hills National Forest. We had covered back roads, I had walked ridges and draws, I had sat under pine trees and tried to call the birds and I was generally worn out from going "into the forest." All would have been mere excuses as far as Jake was concerned. I got the sense that he believed someday he would have to show me how to do it right.

And, of course, he was right. I could have done more. I could have worked harder. I could have gone to more places. I could have done a better job of calling the gobblers with my box call.

My response to Jake was to laugh and tell him he was right. Had the same admonition, "If you want to get a turkey you have to go into the forest," been advanced by a veteran hunter I might have developed a more serious sense of inadequacy and failure. I would have begun to feel that I was lazy afoot and ignorant about the habits of the wild turkey. I might have concluded that just as golf is a good way to ruin a nice walk, so turkey hunting is a prime way to ruin a three-day outing in the Black Hills.

Those words, "you should have," whether stated or implied, are not usually very pleasant words to hear. They back us into a corner and we either just hang our heads or we become defensive, sometimes even defiant.

I recalled this conversation with Jake one week when I was dealing with two Biblical texts having to do with the call of the Old Testament prophet, Isaiah, and the call of one of Jesus' leading disciples, Simon Peter.

Isaiah received his call in the temple. As he sat there in that place so full of symbols he felt the room was full of God's presence. He heard the seraphs praising God, calling one to another and saying, "Holy, holy, holy is the Lord of hosts; the whole earth is full of his glory." It caused Isaiah to feel hopelessly lost and unclean. "Woe is me!" he cried, "I am lost, for I am a man of unclean lips, and I live among a people of unclean lips; yet my eyes have seen the King, the Lord of hosts!" (*Isaiah* 6:1-5) All of the "should haves" Isaiah could think of smothered him.

When Jesus called Peter to be a disciple he also brought Peter to his knees. Peter and his partners had been fishing all night with no luck. Their boat was on the shore and they were washing their nets, perhaps making small talk and longing for a nap. Then Jesus came and asked Peter if he could use his boat, so as to put some distance between himself and the pressing crowds that followed him. He put out a ways, sat down in the boat and continued teaching the people. Then he told Peter to take his boat out to the deep water, let down those clean nets and catch some fish. "That's what we were doing all night, with no luck," Peter protested. He must have been thinking about the same thing we would have thought: "Jesus, we are professional fisherman and you are a carpenter and you are telling us how to catch fish?" But, whatever his musings may have been, he was also a good sport. What's more, Jesus had cured his mother in law of a fever so Peter owed him one. "If you say so," he answered.

The results were unbelievable. They hauled up enough fish to fill not only Peter's boat but his friends' boat too. Peter was astounded—and convicted too. "Go away from me, Lord, for I am a sinful man!" he begged. Jesus could have read the entire law of Moses to Peter and it would not have had as much clout as simply being out fished by Jesus. Peter understood this kind of talk. It brought his guilt and sense of inadequacy to the surface. All his other failures came back to accuse him. It was a big "should have."

It so happened that a few days after my first telephone conversation with Jake I had a second one. His mother and dad had bought him a new bat and ball. They had been pitching to him and he was learning to hit the ball—from time to time. He had to tell me about this new and exhilarating sport called baseball. He asked if I could come up and play ball with him. "It's ok," he assured me, "if you make a mistake."

I suspect he had heard these words from his parents who observed that he often missed the ball. Maybe he had said them to himself too. But now he was assuring me that I did not need to be perfect to play with him. He would, if not overlook, at least forgive my mistakes. It was a graceful invitation. He would cut me some slack.

That's about how it turned out for Isaiah and Peter too.

One of those seraphs flew to Isaiah and touched his lips with a live coal from the altar. "Now that this has touched your lips, your guilt has departed and your sin is blotted out," the seraph promised. Then Isaiah heard a voice saying, "Whom shall I send and who will go for us? He said, "Here I am; send me." And God sent him.

Peter, too, heard a word of grace. "Do not be afraid," Jesus told him, "from now on you will be catching people." There was enough love and challenge in those words to last a lifetime. So Peter put his boat back on the shore. Then he walked away from it and everything else connected with his old job and followed Jesus into an unknown future. And what a future it was.

We all have to deal with a lot of "should haves." We have done things that were wrong and failed to do things that would have been right. Faced with these sins of commission and sins of omission we are troubled and convicted. How can God like us, much less use us, we wonder? What's to become of us, now and in eternity, we ask?

But God has the last word. "It's ok if you have made mistakes," God says. "I will forgive you," God promises, "and I can use you, just as you are." What a gift this is, to know in our hearts that God uses those "should haves" not to hold us down but rather to cause us to look to him rather than ourselves for the strength to go on. And, further, he promises us that the "going on" will be under his direction and care. Isaiah's lips, touched by God, spoke eloquently. Peter became the Big Fisherman, bringing people into the Kingdom of God, rather than fish into his boat, all because it was ok to make mistakes.

Not long ago we had a blizzard and the person in charge of the church office staff where I work called the workers to tell them the office would be closed for the day and they would not have to come to work. Of course that did not apply to the custodians. They come to work regardless of the weather. One of them, John by name, was outside blowing snow off the sidewalk. His glasses were covered with fog and snow so he took them off. He noticed a woman coming from the parking lot across the street and heading for the church. He was not seeing well and she was bundled up so he mistook her for one of the secretaries. He yelled at her, "DIDN'T YOU GET THE CALL?" As it turned out, she was a stranger headed for some other place.

It occurred to me that it would not be a bad idea to have John stand out there every Sunday and yell at the folks coming out of church, "DIDN'T YOU GET THE CALL?"

For it is not only those with famous Biblical names like Isaiah and Peter who are called to serve in some unique capacity. Every believer is called to believe and share his or her life according to the gifts and abilities given by God. That makes the calls to Isaiah and Peter more than historical oddities. It makes them examples of what can happen to us.

An Old Friend

When the chores were done and supper finished, amidst the clatter of grandma's cleanup in the kitchen (hey, this was 50 years ago when grandmas both washed and wiped the dishes, then swept the floor—for the sheer enjoyment of it all!), my grandfather and I would head for the back stoop. The back steps, leading into the shanty, were like bleachers overlooking the pasture and creek, with a splendid view of the western sky. There we would sit, he with his gurgling pipe and I with a good feeling about being his sole companion and "confidant." This was a time for small talk and large silences, the latter coming easier for my grandfather.

The long, silent spaces in our conversation were filled with the melancholy antiphons of the mourning doves and the lilting evensong of the robins. Recently milked cows vocally expressed their pleasure in being released from their burden of milk and the confinement of the stanchions in the barn. A couple of cats usually presented their arched backs to our outstretched hands. They filled the silence with purring as we stroked them. My dog, Brownie, punctuated each change of position with a resigned yawn. These were the quiet sounds of evening vespers on the farm. Then darkness settled in.

On a calm night we could hear the neighbors talking a quarter of a mile away. Through the darkness we could hear the barking of dogs from twice that distance. An owl tuned up for the night's hunt. Crickets began fiddling, likely just for the fun of it. We could hear the slightest of breezes slipping through the big cottonwoods. In the darkness our hearing seemed to be fully engaged. When we took the lantern and walked to the barn, the final phase of the evening ritual, our crunching footsteps sounded twice as loud as they did during the day.

The night lingered on, growing progressively more silent. Then it was time to go to bed and sleep, lulled by the murmurs of darkness.

Simon and Garfunkle began one of their unforgettable songs with the lyrics, "Hello darkness, my old friend, I've come to talk with you again." Most of us are reserved enough not to have talked with the darkness, but we may have done our share of listening to the night.

Audio impressions are most vivid at night. During the day we rely heavily on our vision, but evening calls us to make a transition to a listening mode. Soon our surroundings will be shrouded in darkness. Our eyes will not serve us well any more. Now we shift from observing the day's sights to hearing the night's sounds. Our hearing quickens.

Evening signals the need for another kind of transition too, if one subscribes to the "left brain/right brain" theory. This concept ascribes different functions to each side of the brain. The left side is the control center for analytical activity. It functions as the director of speech and logical thinking. It likes abstractions.

The right side of the brain controls artistic and emotional activity. It is aware of shapes and shades. It fosters feelings and imagination. It likes stories and pictures.

During the day we are apt to favor the left side of the brain as we solve problems, make plans, organize things, figure the angles and measure the results.

But evening, signaling the approach of darkness, invites us to yield to the right side of our brain. Darkness is a time for warm and small talk, reading or watching stories, listening to music, pursuing a hobby or indulging in other forms of coziness. It is a time to savor comfortable feelings. It may also offer a pleasurable moment to listen to the sounds of the night outdoors, especially if you have a back porch and a grandfather to share it with.

In Shakespeare's *Merchant of Venice* the young lovers, Lorenzo and Jessica, are united. Lorenzo leads Jessica out into the night and says,

> "How sweet the moonlight sleeps upon the bank!
> Here will we sit, and let the sounds of music
> Creep in our ears: soft stillness and the night
> Become the touches of sweet harmony."

When shared with others, it is more difficult to remain strangers in the night than in the day. We go deeper in thought and become less superficial in conversation. It is a time for making and cultivating relationships, for feeling close to others.

Night adds mystery to life. As a youngster I used to like watching the daily train come into Oldham at night. It didn't stay long. The doors of the mail car were usually open, and you could see the workers inside wearing pistols. That brought on all kinds of thoughts of train robberies and other exciting wild-west happenings. You could see the people sitting in the passenger car, people whom you had never seen before and would never see again. I wondered where they had come from and where they were going. They were there, in my hometown, for an instant and then they were gone—into the night. The sounds of migrating geese going overhead at night left me with the same kind of feeling, a mixture of wonder and curiosity, with maybe a touch of melancholy. I suppose I had come up against the mysterious and transitory nature of life itself, although as a kid I couldn't identify the thought.

Of all the emotions triggered by darkness I suppose fear would be pretty close to the top, given the right circumstances. Who hasn't been afraid of the dark? As an adult I confess I am not quite free from that fear. Who knows what might be lurking out there? After all, it is a time when our imagination is strong. In the inner city, fear of the dark is a totally rational fear. But where I have lived it is mostly irrational. I know there is really nothing out there to be afraid of, but I still walk a little faster by the lonely places at night.

There is one reference in the Bible that captures my gratitude for the darkness. In *Psalm 42:8* we read, "By day the Lord commands his steadfast love, and at night his song is with me, a prayer to the

God of my life." The light of day provides ample opportunities at home and on the job, at work and at play, alone or with others, to pursue our ambitions and channel our energies. But at night we can relax into the care of God, savoring life's softer qualities and its richness. It is a time of rest and trust. It is supremely the time to let God be God.

Hello darkness, our old friend!

The Rescue

One spring day when my father came home spattered with mud from head to toe I knew it had not been an average day for him. Moreover, he displayed a bit of a fluster, which was not character-istic of him. I was about eleven at the time, and I guess he thought I deserved an explanation. I think he needed to explain the whole episode to himself too.

It had started with a call from a woman whose husband--we'll call him "Sam"--had taken up more or less permanent residence in the bar that afternoon. This was not the first time Sam had languished in the local watering hole, and his wife knew what the results would likely be. She asked my father to do her the favor of going down to the bar, getting Sam out and taking him home before he drank himself into a stupor.

That was not a welcome or easy assignment. Dad was a proper person. A favorite memory of mine is one of him working in the garden, in dress shirt and tie under his blousy coverall. Cavorting with drunks was not his favorite pastime. Moreover he had no idea of what kind of reception he would receive from either Sam or his drinking buddies. He did not think Sam would be very receptive to this plan hatched by his wife and implemented by the local pastor. He hoped the confrontation would not be too dramatic.

But Sam obliged. Seeing the pastor, who had never been in the bar before, walk in the front door and head for him made him mellow and accommodating. Everybody else, some of them no doubt church members too, backed away. The two unlikely companions left the bar together.

They settled into my father's car for the drive out into the country. The roads were soft and slippery from recent spring rains. The last one half mile to Sam's place was the most treacherous of all. It was one of those prairie tracks with no gravel or ditches, the kind of road we always took when we were road hunting for pheasants. Predictably, they became stuck in one of the grassy shoulders.

Dad's options were limited. Sam had been in his cups too long and was in no condition to get out and push. His driving skills were also greatly impaired but there was no traffic to worry about. The worst he could do might be to take out a fence post or two and bury the car in a plowed field.

So my father got out of the car and had Sam slide behind the steering wheel. He put his weight behind the car, yelled "ok" and waited for the signal to reach Sam's foot. Sam roared the engine and dad heaved forward. Mud flew everywhere. The car eased out of the grassy rut back on to the road. Not wanting to stop the car on that slippery stretch of road, my father jumped into the passenger side. Sam rose to the challenge and aimed the car toward home. It was not the first time he had driven in that condition. He brought the car to a halt in front of his house.

Sam's wife came to the front door and stared at the dirty vehicle in disbelief. She had requested the pastor to bring her shaky husband home. It appeared that the reverse had happened. Sam, it seemed, had delivered the pastor to her home. Sam sat behind the wheel, clean and composed, appearing to be in command of the situation. The pastor sat next to him, out of breath, red in the face, covered with mud and wearing a sheepish grin

It was not immediately clear to her who was the chauffeur and who was the chauffeured.

It was shortly after that improbable scene when dad arrived home and provided me with a breathy explanation of what had happened. By then he had begun to see the humor of it all. Of course, he had no idea that his son would some day turn it into a parable with spiritual ramifications.

The Heavenly Father dispatched Jesus into this world to rescue people from various forms of self-destruction. To do so Jesus went to all kinds of people in all kinds of places. He came to them and offered to help. He invited them to come with him, and he would show them their true home. He called it the Kingdom of God.

To accomplish his mission Jesus allowed himself to be humiliated and abused. He got plenty of mud on his face. The prophet Isaiah, hundreds of years earlier, painted a poetic, word picture of what Jesus would have to endure to fulfill his task:

> "He had no form or majesty that we should
>   look at him,
> nothing in his appearance that we should
>   desire him.
>
> He was despised and rejected by others;
>   a man of suffering and acquainted
>   with infirmity;
> and as one from whom others hide their faces
>   he was despised, and we held him
>   of no account.
>
> But he was wounded for our transgressions,
>   crushed for our iniquities;
> upon him was the punishment that made us whole,
>   and by his bruises we are healed.
>
> All we like sheep have gone astray;
>   we have all turned to our own way,
> and the Lord has laid on him the iniquity
>   of us all." (*Isaiah* 53: 2-3, 5-6)

In the end he was made to look ridiculous. Prior to his crucifixion the soldiers fitted him with a colorful robe and placed on his head a crown of thorns. They shouted mock tributes, "hail king!" They had their laughs and when they tired of this pathetic hilarity they nailed him to a cross. But they could not quite let it go. "If you're a king, save yourself," they taunted. When he told them he was thirsty, their idea of a practical joke was to lift a sponge full of sour wine to his face.

From all appearances you would think it was Jesus who needed to be rescued. Those whom he came to save seem to be very much in control. All of them, those who shouted "crucify him, crucify him," those who worked behind the scenes to bring him to destruction, Pilate, Herod, the soldiers and all who gave assent by their silence, went home to a nice meal, some playtime with the kids and a good night's rest. And, on a hill outside of town, Jesus gasped for his next breath.

But now we see, through the eyes of faith, that it was Jesus who did the rescuing. As composed as we might appear, as much in control as we might imagine ourselves to be, we are headed for destruction without him. John states it better than most: "To as many as received him, who believed in his name, he gave power to become the children of God." *(John* 1:12)

So when Jesus interrupts our self-centered activities and asks us to come with him because he wants to take us to our rightful home—the Kingdom of God—it may be a good idea to go with him.

Trouble In The Grove

My grandfather's ritual of haying began in the grove, north of the house. He would lug a six-foot sickle up to his pedal grindstone in the shade of the many trees. Before he started sharpening he always filled the tin can that hung above the stone with water. The can had a hole in the bottom with a string hanging down in order to direct the drops of water down to the grindstone. Then he would climb on board and sit there, peddling away, balancing the sickle on the rotating stone like he was riding a bicycle across a high wire. A little shot of tobacco juice now and then would provide extra lubrication for the sharpening process. When the sickle was sharp he would fit it into the mower, hitch up his team of blacks, Prince and Bill, and head for the hay meadow.

Picking a day for mowing hay was not a decision he left to himself. He listened carefully to Whitey Larson on WNAX in Yankton for direction. Whitey knew his audience and would spend a good deal of time providing the weather forecast as a part of his news program. Instead of saying it would be a warm and sunny day, he would encourage the women to do their washing and the farmers to mow the hay. Whitey was colorful and folksy. He had a large audience, including my grandparents.

During the first cutting of the year my grandfather would some-times run over a pheasant nest. Usually the hen pheasant would escape the sickle. But not always. On one occasion, when the pheasant had not eluded the sickle, my grandfather gathered up the eggs, took them home and placed them under a "clucking" hen, which I understood to mean a chicken in a motherly mood.

After the pheasant chicks hatched, the mother chicken proudly squired her brood around the farm. At first they clustered around her as though it was a natural arrangement. But as they grew they became increasingly independent and skittish. Soon the wildness in them took over completely and they scattered into the fields. My grandfather remembered watching the surrogate mama frantically chasing the chicks through the grove, trying to keep up with them. She wanted to know where they were going. She wanted them back. Eventually she gave up and resumed her quiet life around the chicken coop. Her family had fled.

The pheasant chicks were too small to be on their own. They had not been schooled on how to find food in the wild and how to elude a variety of predators. Probably most did not survive.

When Jesus approached Jerusalem for the last time he paused outside the city to contemplate the way things had gone. He had a few followers and had aroused the curiosity of many more. His mis-sion was to bring the Kingdom of God to people so that God could establish his kingly rule and bring grace and love to them.

He gave the invitation but so many had spurned it. Now as he neared the great city on the hill he looked sadly at the glittering temple. It was a place of worship but the one to be worshiped remained largely unknown to the people. They had rejected him.

> "Jerusalem, Jerusalem, the city that kills the prophets and stones those who are sent to it! How often have I desired to gather your children together as a hen gath-ers her brood under her wings, and you were not will-ing! See, your house is left to you, desolate." (*Matthew* 23:37,38)

The words of Jesus throb with a feeling of rejection. If only they would accept. But they would not.

Their rejection of God's invitation was actually a form of rebel-lion. Jesus came to the chosen people, after all. God had claimed these people as his possession. "You are mine," God had said. God had blessed them so that they might become a blessing to others. God intended that they should be a servant people. They were uninterested.

We all understand this form of rebellion. Those of us who have been gathered up and placed under the guardianship of the Lord are prone to dash off into the fields of our own choosing. Sometimes we do it because we are distracted and gradually forget God. We are like the sheep that never consciously set out to leave the shepherd but just put its head down and, going from one tuft of grass to another, ate its way away. At other times we rise up and deliberately declare to God, "I'll do it my way." Like the prodigal son we long to shake ourselves free from the dominance of our Father and get away to a "far country" where we can be on our own.

The consequences of our rebellion are serious. "The wages of sin," Paul declares, "are death." I'm not sure this is a threat as much as it is a statement of fact. Having fled from God's care we let go of our lifeline, through which faith, hope and love come to us. These spiritual gifts may not be necessary to keep our hearts beating, but they are a requirement for any kind of life remotely described as spiritual. They elevate us from the primal level of existence to the joyous level of life.

But there is a strong word in the Bible that makes all the difference in the world. It is the word "return." It is a call to repentance. The Old Testament prophet, Isaiah, proclaimed:

> "Seek the Lord while he may be found
> Call upon him while he is near;
> Let the wicked forsake their way,
> And the unrighteous their thoughts;
> Let them return to the Lord,
> That he may have mercy on them,
> And to our God, for he will abundantly pardon."
> (*Isaiah*.55:6,7)

The good word "return" is sounded for those who have run away from God, which includes all of us from time to time. It is not a word tossed out lightly. It is a word of promise and love.

Return to what? Not, surely, to a vengeful God. Not to a God who has a score to settle with us. Not even to a God who is going to send us to the corner of the room. The word "return" is an invitation to return to a God whose heart is overflowing with love. I sometimes think God may have the most compassion for those who are weak and made mistakes because of that weakness.

My grandfather's designated hen mother had no choice but to watch her tiny flock of pheasant chicks run away. I suppose, in her own fowl way, she ached for them to return. But she was powerless to stop them or retrieve them.

It is not so with God. Surely God will not force us into the orbit of his care. But God comes looking for us when we take flight. That is really the essence of Christmas. We get our first glimpse of a God who comes searching for us in order to bring us back under the shadow of her wing.

Vic

In 1965 I came back to my home state of South Dakota after wandering in the far countries of Kansas, Colorado, Minnesota and Wisconsin. Vic was one of the first persons I met at East Side Lutheran Church, where I was called to be Youth Pastor. He, too, hailed from Oldham, my hometown, and I knew several of his family very well. But I had not met Vic before. I still remember the first time I saw him sitting in the church basement against the east wall, bent over a cup of coffee, chatting with fellow members of the congregation. The occasion was a reception to welcome my family and me to East Side. Because of the old hometown and family ties I went over to greet him. That marked the beginning of a friendship that lasted twenty-five years. We swapped many stories, spent time in each other's homes, teamed up on many hunting adventures and, with our families, traveled to Alaska together.

Vic was a big, strong man. My sons remember that he never wore more than thin cotton gloves, even on the coldest of days. For his size he was exceptionally mobile. I often struggled to keep up with him when we hunted out in the Black Hills. He loved to hunt, mainly, I think, because he was so at home in the out of doors. It was Vic who got me hooked on turkey hunting. We did all the others too, but the turkey hunting was something special. There is a unique challenge to turkey hunting and when you combine that with the warming weather of spring in the beauty of the Black Hills you have a winning combination.

Besides being a man of deep faith and character Vic had a wonderful sense of humor. He had a quick wit and was a great teller of stories. If I close my eyes and listen carefully I can still hear his rich laughter beginning in short, fitful bursts and then erupting in great peals. Most often, though, his humor was subtle, consisting of one-liners that he delivered in an off-handed way, as though he did not intend to produce comedy.

My boys will not forget the frigid night north of Bison, So. Dak. We were all as cold as ice cubes. As we crawled into the backs of our pickups and slipped into our sleeping bags I overheard Vic mutter to one of my sons, "Be sure to remind me we're having fun." It was an old line but Vic made it sound fresh and funny, temporarily distracting us from our discomfort.

Another time several of us were hunting turkeys in the early spring in the Black Hills. We slept on mattresses at a local church and then rose at three a.m. in order to get out into the Hills before daybreak. As we groggily trudged back and forth to the bathroom I met Vic in the hallway. His comment, "It doesn't take long to stay overnight here," pretty much woke me up.

Vic and his wife, Florence, together with another couple, often came to help us observe special occasions in our family—graduations, confirmations, weddings and the like. I have a vivid image of the four of them parking across the street from our home in Watertown. As they walked toward our house George held out a large paper sack. "I brought you some tomatoes," he said. I peeked into the sack and saw a hefty bottle of what many in my profession use only for medicinal purposes. As I responded with a pleased, but surprised expression, Vic quipped, "You should see his cucumbers."

Our most improbable adventure took place in Shannon County on a deer hunt. Vic shot a deer on the other side of a fairly high and fast moving stream. Initially we had crossed over on a bridge way downstream. But we did not wish to drag the deer back that far. So we did the next best thing. We divested ourselves of boots, socks, shorts and pants and floated the deer across. It was a hilarious moment. We agreed that if the wrong person had come by at the wrong moment and witnessed these two semi-nude hunters with their floating deer we might have gained a reputation we neither coveted nor deserved.

When Vic passed away it was like the toppling of an oak. It left a gaping hole in my woodlot of friends. I am grateful to have shared so many experiences with him and for his example of how humor can lift our spirits.

Laughter is one of those ingredients in life that we take for granted. It is so much around us that we hardly ever imagine what life would be like without it. Evidently Martin Luther had given it some notice because he said, "If you're not allowed to laugh in heaven, I don't want to go there." He may have been thinking of the personal pleasure that comes from laughing. Or, on the other hand, he may have been thinking he did not wish to spend an eternity in an environment where others had no sense of humor. Even a fishing trip, to say nothing of eternity, with companions unable to laugh or bring others to laughter would be miserable. Hell has often been portrayed as a fiery misery but it would be nearly as grim if it were pictured as a place of utter boredom and sobriety—with no humor whatsoever.

In his book, *The Humor of Christ*, Elton Trueblood tells about Sir Arthur Quiller-Couch who said, in one of his University of Cambridge lectures, "I suppose that if an ordinary man of my age were asked which has better helped him to bear the burs of life— religion or a sense of humor—he would, were he quite honest, be perplexed for an answer." His point was that the person with a sense of humor is one who has more than a battery of jokes; he has a coping mechanism that serves him even in the middle of trouble.

Indeed humor seems to be an integral part of trouble or misfortune. Consider the history of American humor, so much of which comes from the Jewish and Black traditions. Both of these groups have known plenty of trouble and their humor has probably been because of rather than in spite of the suffering they have experienced. Humor has helped them cope.

I'm reminded of an incident that took place at my mother's funeral. Erik, our youngest son, was only six years old at the time. We stood huddled together at the cemetery as the pastor brought the committal service to a conclusion. Erik suddenly put up both hands to cover his ears as the pastor began the words of the benediction, "The Lord bless you and keep you . . ." I bent over and asked Erik why he was covering his ears. "They're going to drop it now," he answered. He had come to recognize those words as a sign of closing and he assumed the final act would be to drop the casket in the grave. In spite of the sadness of the moment I had to chuckle at his misunderstanding. Mother probably would have hooted. To extract a note of humor from her funeral would have been exactly what she would have wanted.

On a personal level many of us have learned to handle our shortcomings, failures and foibles by making light of them and laughing at ourselves. It beats crying. We are human and must contend daily with all the flaws our humanity entails. Laughter helps us not to take ourselves too seriously. Without it we might be overcome with feelings of frustration or despair. Without it we might have to devise some other way of dealing with our weaknesses—like blaming others. So we strive to cultivate that kind of inner security which allows us to laugh at ourselves and, in effect, says, "this is who I am, take me or leave me." Besides helping us to cope with ourselves, it makes us better friends and neighbors too. We are saying, "I'm not perfect and you don't have to be perfect either."

Those persons we have known who have helped us see the funny side of life are special blessings to us. It would be difficult to overestimate their contribution. My thoughts of that special person, Vic, simply remind me that I am surrounded by people who are able to bring humor out of the most complex and simple situations. I hope, with their help and God's help, to keep laughing right up to the last day.

Load Limits

My grandfather fired up his old Chrysler with the curtains in the back windows about three times a week, once for church and twice to drive to Garretson. The weekday trips to Garretson were for the purpose of delivering cream and eggs and returning with whatever groceries and dry goods were needed for the sustenance of life.

Occasionally grandma would ride along, either to just get out of the house or because she did not quite trust my grandfather to get the right goods.

It was about a three and a half mile jaunt. Coming from the west, as we did, meant we had to cross the bridge over the Split Rock River on the edge of town. On either side of the bridge there was a sign declaring the maximum load limit to be something like 10,000 lbs.

Almost always my grandfather would turn to me and with a twinkle in his eye say, "Well we'd better let grandma out or we won't make it." He would slow down as though he was going to stop. Grandma, who was decidedly overweight, took the teasing good-not naturally, especially since she knew the humor was for my benefit. She would laugh and mockingly threaten, "you do that and I might not get back in again."

In the spring the county would also put load limit signs on some of the soggy gravel roads around my hometown of Oldham. Later, in the summer, when the roads dried the signs would be removed. My father never joked with my mother about getting out. She was of average weight and also far more weight conscious than my grandmother. Her response would not have been to laugh!

I believe load limits have a far wider application than just for bridges or gravel roads. I think humans have load limits too.

One could interpret the American Revolution as a case of the English exceeding the load limits of the American colonists. The colonists eventually rebelled against the heavy handedness of the English. It came to a head with the Boston Tea Party.

The English parliament granted the East India Company the exclusive right to monopolize the tea trade in America. When, in 1773, that company placed an unreasonable duty on tea, a band of Americans, disguised as Indians, boarded the company's ships. They dumped all of the tea into Boston Harbor. They were protesting taxation without representation and the threat of a few companies favored by the crown monopolizing American commerce and industry.

The colonists refused to bear up under the weight of British colonialism. One wonders what might have happened if the English had proceeded more cautiously and fairly and paid some attention to the tolerance level of the Americans.

There are spiritual dimensions to this business of a load limit too. When Jesus sent out his twelve disciples he described their mission and issued a warning. He dispatched them in pairs and granted them authority over unclean spirits. He asked them to observe a load limit. He ordered them to take nothing for their journey except a staff. They would not need cash, bread or a bag. His reasoning may have been that if you have an empty bag you soon develop a shopper's mentality. You want to fill it with items. He told them to wear sandals and one tunic, in contrast to the fashion of the day, which was to wear an outer and an inner tunic. On their journey they were not to be burdened with concerns of either property or propriety.

Nor were they to harbor grudges, always a heavy load for any person to carry. If the village they entered did not provide the expected hospitality, a sacred duty in the East, he instructed them to shake off the dust on their feet and move on. Don't make an issue of it, he seems to say, and don't labor under the crippling spell of injured feelings or denied rights. Being too easily offended might put them off their course of calling for repentance and healing the sick.

Their mission was too grand to be encumbered with a host of practical concerns that would inevitably alter their focus. In simplifying their lives they would learn to trust in God's care and find their fulfillment in the glory of their mission.

One naturally draws a comparison between those disciples and us. Times and conditions have changed. It would not only be impractical but also impossible to literally follow those instructions today. Alas, there are salaries, pensions, medical benefits, insurance policies, investments and social security matters to consider these days. And, while our closets may not be packed with the latest fashions, for the sake of our colleagues we need to observe some variety in dress. Nor can you just move in with another family and stay there indefinitely. Your hosts, and others who feared they might become hosts, would soon propose some sort of housing allowance. And, while you might prefer not to carry much money in your purse or billfold, you had better have a working credit card or checkbook within reach.

Yet, the principles of simplicity and respecting one's personal load limit when it comes to the practical aspects of living are as important now as they were then.

Jesus pointed to the cares of this world as a heavy burden. One still needs to slice through the clutter of one's life to find what is central and basic. We set aside a fraction of our week to come to church for worship. It is a time to zero in on the deepest meanings of life, when much that is extraneous to life can be at least temporarily shelved. Worship puts into focus, like nothing else, our identity and destiny.

Worries, too, can sometimes exceed our load limit. God knows there is enough to worry about; finances, health, children and work would head the list. Even our marriage liturgy recognizes this reality by acknowledging that the "gift of family can become a burden."

But the solution is not to worry that we worry too much. It is rather to accept the invitation extended by Peter, "Cast all your anxiety on him, because he cares for you." (I *Peter* 5:7) Peter may have had in mind one of the most wonderful promises ever given to us by Jesus. It is a promise full of understanding and feeling, altogether tender and loving: "Come to me, all you that are weary and are carrying heavy burdens, and I will give you rest. Take my yoke upon you, and learn from me; for I am gentle and humble in heart, and you will find rest for your souls. For my yoke is easy, and my burden is light." (*Matthew* 11:28-30)

Bridges and roads are not built to carry excessive loads. There are limits and they are often posted for our safety.

People, too, have load limits. Too much clutter in our lives can pile up and block out the light of God's glory. Too many cares and worries can pull us down into the mire of misery. Jesus always couples his warnings about our load limits with the grand promise to lift the burdens and set us free to dance.

Max

Max did everything with pizzazz, including dying. His goal in life was to "live it to the max," which he did. As a senior at Roosevelt High School he played tennis, served as Student Council President and generally provided a lift to everyone he met. More than once I met him while I was out walking. He would be cruising in his purple Mitsubishi with the speakers thumping and I would be on the receiving end of a blast from his horn and a friendly wave and smile.

Max had battled leukemia as a six year old. After a series of treatments he was determined to be cancer free. So the next twelve years were good years. Max was filled with life. He had a great many friends, the most winsome smile you will ever encounter and an outgoing style that took everybody in. As a fourteen year old he attended my ninth grade confirmation class. Surrounded by friends, he was not always focused on the task at hand and I had to rein in his gregarious tendencies from time to time. But he could also ask some great questions and, even though he sometimes seemed not to be listening, could provide pointed summaries of what we had talked about. I had no doubt that he knew what the Christian Faith was all about and that he had a personal trust in the Lord.

Then the cancer returned, though there is some reason to believe it was a totally different brand of leukemia. Max was a junior at the time and spent much of the second half of his junior year in Rochester. The treatments were brutal and left Max in terrible shape. But he rebounded and entered his senior year with his usual gusto. This time, though, there was no sense of being free of cancer. It was there and it began its comeback soon. Max eventually decided enough was enough. No more treatments! A number of last-ditch opportunities to travel here or there for rumored cures were presented but he turned them down, much to the dismay of those who were willing to try anything to save him.

Now he gradually shaped two goals in his mind and they became life-sustaining inspiration for him. His first goal was to graduate from Roosevelt High School. I have his senior picture posted in my office and besides that winning smile there is a look of determination in his eyes, as though he is thinking, "Take my word for it, I'm going to graduate." And he did.

The second goal was to go to heaven. I have known a number of people who, while still alive, had one foot in the grave. But I can't recall anyone else for whom heaven was as real and welcome as it was for Max. Towards the end he really had one foot in heaven.

We had been trying to get together for a visit for some time but Max's calendar was jammed and I told him to give me a call when he found some time. One day, when I was in the midst of cleaning my garage, Max called. He asked if he could come over. We pulled up a couple of folding chairs in my garage, sipped on cokes and talked about life, death and heaven. He wanted to know what I knew about heaven. I was not very helpful in that the Bible does not go into detailed descriptions of what heaven is like. But that did not dampen Max's enthusiasm for going there. He thought of heaven in terms of relationships, which is quite proper I think. He was anxious to see his deceased grandfather again. He looked forward to meeting Jesus. He was so ready to go to heaven that he told me if he were offered a chance to be completely healed he did not think he would accept it. Max found so much to his liking in this life that he was confident God would provide something even greater in the next one. Before he left he stepped in the house to tell my wife good-by. Max drove off in his purple car and I returned to my garage, sensing that it was now a holy place.

Max's health gradually deteriorated and he began to slip quickly after his graduation party, which had been a lively one. A few days thereafter I was called over to his house on a Saturday night. Max was in bed, surrounded by family and friends. He welcomed me with a big smile. We chatted for awhile and then he asked if I would read aloud a poem he had written. I said I would and half way through it wondered if I would make it to the end. As his buddies, girlfriend and family stood around the bed I read his poem, one that he described as "From My Heart."

"Last night I spoke to Jesus
Though I couldn't quite understand.
He told me that he needed me,
And soon I would hold his hand.
I told him I wasn't ready to go so soon,
And kept asking him why.
All I remember him saying is,
"You will be an angel in the sky."

Last night I spoke to Jesus,
His voice was nice and calm.
He told me he was getting ready,
And that it wouldn't be that long.
I asked him about my grandpa,
And the ones that went before.
He told me that they were waiting,
And will be there at heaven's door.

Last night I spoke to Jesus,
And now I understand.
Why he said that he needed me,
And I would soon hold his hand.
There is a special task above,
That now I must go complete.
But my friends that's not the end,
Because some day soon we will all meet.

Though I must leave you all behind,
I will be in your hearts everyday.
And when your time has come,
I will be there to help you find the way.
Last night I spoke to Jesus,
And he told me that there will be tears.

Just remember the memories,
Over the past couple years.

My life may have been short,
But filled with so much love.
And often you ask Jesus why,
He takes such young children
    From us to put up above.
Soon some day you will walk the path and see,
That leaving this earth is all a part of a victory.
And when God needs you above
    And not on earth anymore,
    I will be waiting for you
In the gateway of heaven's door."

During the night Max slipped into a coma and by the time we concluded church on Sunday I received a call that he had passed away.

Though Max was a member of Peace Lutheran we held his funeral at First Lutheran in order to accommodate the crowd. The church was packed. Max's casket was covered with messages scrawled by his friends. In the sermon I challenged other youth to pick up the slack left by Max's passing. Who would assume responsibility for student government? Who would flash that friendly smile now at those who needed to be affirmed? Who could find ways to demonstrate the role of faith for young people? How could all of us find ways to live life to the max?

Max's brother led the way to the cemetery in Max's purple Mitsubishi. At the graveside friends released a bevy of balloons. As they soared skyward we had a sense of Max's victory over death. I have returned on several occasions to Max's grave and it is amazing to find all of the articles of affection young people have left there, including a small replica of the purple car.

The English poet, Alfred E. Housman, in his poem, "To an Athlete Dying Young," described the early death of a young hero: "The time you won your town the race we chaired you through the market place . . .." he begins. But now the youth has died and he is being borne through the streets "shoulder high" to a "stiller town." Housman continues,

"Smart lad, to slip betimes away
    From fields where glory does not stay,

And early though the laurel grows
It withers quicker than the rose...Now you will not
swell the rout
Of lads that wore their honors out,
Runners whom renown outran
And the name died before the man."

I am not sure that A.E. Housman ever lost a son. And the young man who died may very well have been willing to exchange his transitory athletic glory for more meaningful adult pursuits and rewards. So, while it may be a thought-provoking poem, I find it to be a bit more provoking than thoughtful.

The death of a promising youth is tragic. I believe God was sad to see it happen. God is always on the side of life and God could have used Max in a variety of ways had he lived. But, the minute Max breathed his last breath, I believe God was there to wrap his divine arms around Max and bring him to a more glorious life. And God will use the enduring memory of Max which many of us hold dearly as a way to remind us that life is to be lived with gusto and when it comes to an end to let it go in the confidence that we are headed for something even better.

OTHER TITLES BY THE AUTHOR:

Prairie Parables

A Road Once Traveled (and other Prairie Parables)

*Additional copies of this or other books
by David Johnson can be obtained from:*

David Johnson
1701 Silver Creek Circle
Sioux Falls, S.D. 57106